GUN TO GUN!

"Go ahead," I told him. "Pick up the gun. Carefully, though, or I'll blow a hole in your guts. I'm gonna give you a fair shake, but we're gonna do it my way. You jest pick it up by the barrel and hold it out at arm's length. Careful now!"

"I don't want to fight you, mister. I ain't no damn fool of a kid. I know what you're plannin' to do. Soon's I have that gun in my hands, you're gonna shoot me and say it happened in self-defense. G'wan! If you're gonna kill me for somethin' I didn't do, then you go on and do it. Shoot me!"

For a moment I was distracted, and he dived to the ground, rolling over with the rifle in his hands. It boomed, and I felt a hot pain lance across my shoulder as I dropped to my knees, triggering the carbine from my hip. . . .

Also by Robert Bell
Published by Ballantine Books:

FEUD AT DEVIL'S RIVER

PLATTE RIVER CROSSING

STRANGER IN DODGE

A VALLEY CALLED DISAPPOINTMENT

NEVER SAY DIE

Robert Bell

BALLANTINE BOOKS • NEW YORK

Library of Congress Catalog Card Number: 85-90710

ISBN 0-345-32502-8

Manufactured in the United States of America

First Edition: August 1985

To my friend, Paul Showalter—Patagonia, Arizona. Paul was a working cowboy for too many years to remember and, while a lawman along the Arizona-Mexican border, earned the respect, and the reputation, that comes with gun-handiness. A friend and adviser to the late John Wayne, Paul is a walking manual of the equipage used in our early West, an engraver, silversmith, and artist who makes fine saddles in his spare time.

PROLOGUE

THE TWO WHITE MEN ATTACKED THE CAMP WITHOUT
warning, one of them smashing Dja-o-aha to the ground with a
heavy wooden club. The Old One wailed, then began keening
his death song as he watched from the shade of a juniper, weakened and helpless from their long journey. His eyes rolled back
until only a portion of the whites showed in the deeply set
sockets. As he rocked back and forth, thin, bony shoulders
twitching in time to his chant, he stared and waited for death to
come.

The woman stood paralyzed with horror, the blankets she'd
taken from the pack sliding unnoticed to the ground. Dazed, her
husband tried to raise up on his arms as blood poured from his
wounded head and trickled from the corners of his mouth.
Cackling with glee, the ragged white man raised the club high
over his head and brought it down with all his strength. A
choked scream was cut off as his victim's back arched and his
toes drummed on the ground. A shudder shook the body, then
stilled. Dja-o-aha, an Apache of the Mimbres band, was dead,
and his killer whooped and danced a jig.

The other man limped slowly toward her, gingerly placing his torn, bleeding feet as if walking on eggs. He held out his hand. "Easy there, missy. I don't aim to hurt you none." A malevolent leer twisted his bearded face, and a lone gold tooth gleamed in the center of his lower jaw. "No, sir! I'd hafta be plumb looney was I to harm a purty thing like you. You jist hold still, now, and don't try nuthin' foolish." A heaviness had come into his voice, and his breathing sounded labored. His hands clenched, then opened, then clenched again as be began to hobble faster, ragged Army pants clinging to his muscled shanks. A sharp rock dug into one lacerated foot, and he stumbled; a curse rasped from his throat as he strove to keep his balance on the rock-strewn ground.

Na-li-igai lunged for the rifle hidden under deerskins a few feet away. One hand grasping the barrel, she worked the lever swiftly, loading a cartridge into the chamber. Without bothering to aim she triggered off a round at the nearest of her enemies, missing but forcing the man to dive for cover. A clump of pinyons beckoned close by, and he scrambled desperately, reaching it just as the woman's second bullet burned across his shoulder. Beyond the clearing, the couple's huge tawny dog lunged at a rawhide leash, snapping and snarling in impotent fury, his claws throwing showers of sand as he scrabbled for purchase in the loose soil.

Hardly pausing, Na-li-igai ran toward the dog, jerking a knife from her belt and then levering up another round. Swiftly, she slashed at the dog's tether and then stepped back as he rushed toward the hidden attacker. Cries of anguish and a wail of terror announced the dog's arrival. A moment later, the man burst from the trees in panic, the dog at his heels.

Her husband's killer had been bent over the body, roughly searching through pockets for something of value. When his partner tried for cover, Na-li-igai's shot urging him along, the smaller man lifted his club and ran at her, soundlessly closing the gap. A thin cry from the Old One made her spin, rifle held at her hip. The muzzle belched flame, and a slug tore the club from the man's hands. Dirty white smoke completely obscured her target as she levered out an empty and reloaded again. By the time she could see, he was gone. A crashing sound in the brush gave a hint as to the direction of his flight, but it was too late. He was out of sight.

No tears stained her face as she stared down at her husband's body, but they would come later; nor did she consider gashing her body or hacking off her fingers. The life that she held deep in her belly would need all her strength.

CHAPTER 1

THAT FIRST WHACK CAUGHT ME RIGHT SQUARE ON the back of my head; about where it joins the neck, and from then on I couldn't move. I tried to get up, or to at least roll away, but I couldn't budge. It was like I was all rubbery, and my arms and legs were numb. Confused and hurting, I wanted to shout *why*, but I couldn't make a sound.

Oh, I could feel the pain, all right. It hurt like hell, and you can believe that! Whatever this feller was smacking me with was heavy, and it drew blood every time he connected. I could feel it running down my face and taste it in my mouth. I tried to lift an arm but couldn't do it.

He never said one word. All I could hear were his grunts and his heavy breathing. Somebody tugged at my boots, and I felt them slipping off; just then another blow struck me right above my ear. It wasn't just one man but two! I felt fingers fumbling with my belt buckle and heard the jingling of chain links clashing together; then I screamed as the thing slashed down the side of my head, smashing into my shoulder and bringing unbearable pain!

Still lying on my side, I tried to focus on my left hand and concentrate on the sounds. I heard the tinkling, and it came clear. A trace chain. He was beating me to death with a trace chain—one of my own, taken from the wagon harness. The beating went on, and pain tore at me while I gritted my teeth to keep from crying out again. A burning rage now, a savage, berserk anger at what was happening. If I survived, I'd hunt those coyotes down if I had to crawl!

Somewhere along the line, a blow from the chain rolled me over on my back, and I peered through the mists of pain at a man standing over me. He was heavily bearded, and his mouth gaped wide open. Moonlight glinted from a solid gold tooth set among broken black snags in his lower jaw. I tried to make out his face, but there wasn't much to see, most of it being covered with hair. He stooped and picked up the holstered Colt revolver I'd placed close to hand, a precaution that wasn't of much use now, considering my helpless condition.

With a grunt of satisfaction, he drew the gun, thumbed it back to half cock, and spun the cylinder to check the loads. The Navy Model, it was, .36-caliber and six-shot, but like a lot of men I'd left one chamber empty for safety's sake.

"A little light," he told me, "but it'll do the job. I'd like to give you time to say a prayer, mister, but we're not all that long on time." Thumbing back the hammer, he pointed toward my head and touched off the trigger.

I saw the flash and screamed as pain seared my shoulder and exploded in my brain. Then the blackness came, that awful, gut-twisting nausea. A taste of copper was in my mouth as I fell, tumbling end over end into a vast, bottomless hole.

CHAPTER 2

∞∞∞∞∞∞∞∞∞∞∞∞∞∞∞∞∞∞∞∞∞∞∞∞∞∞∞∞∞∞∞∞∞∞∞∞∞

An anxious whine and a cold nose woke me from the dead; a long, hard pull it was, too. Seemed like I was clawing up a high hill that stretched up . . . up . . . up, almost to where I could see a single bright star over my head. Each move was an agony of unbearable pain, but I had to reach the ridge of that hill or stay dead forever. I reached out a hand, trying to grab a handhold on the star, and felt the knots in my belly, tasted the bile as it rose in my throat.

I just can't do it. Hurts too much! C'mon, you gotta try, hombre! One step at a time. Don't give up. Never say die! You can do it. Now! See there, I told you you'd make it. Getting closer, now. Sky's coming light, and it ain't far now. I'll make it or my name's not Jake Bailey!

Rolling over, I drew up one leg and managed to get on my knees with one foot planted solidly on the ground. It felt strange, and looking down, I saw that I was barefoot. Head spinning, I wavered there for a moment. I was so weak. Palms on the ground, I made an attempt to stand, but it wasn't all that easy. I was too weak, and my head was spinning. Overbalanced, I fell, sprawling, and that blackness came again.

Minutes or hours later I found myself on my back, looking into the warm brown eyes of a dog. He was whining and shoving at my face and neck with a moist nose.

Experimenting, I found that I could open and close my hands; that was a real feat in itself, since they were torn and bloody, with one of my fingers bent at an angle. I guessed that I'd tried to block a blow from the chain, but I didn't remember even moving.

Next, I tried bending my arms, both at the elbow and at the wrist. Everything worked so far. Now all I had to do was stand, but I was going to need some help. If I got close to a tree, maybe I could pull myself to my feet. The clearing where I'd made my camp was a small one, surrounded by mostly scrub growth, juniper and pinyon, none of them being quite tall. But they were tough and springy and would serve the purpose if I could get close to one.

Carefully, I turned my head, not really sure my neck wasn't broken from the way it hurt. I could hear water in the creek, and right away I got awful thirsty. Standing up just had to wait until I got me a drink of water.

Once more I rolled over and got to my knees. The dog whined and pranced toward me, thinking it was some kind of a game. He barked, and suddenly I felt the warmest feeling of not being alone. Whose dog he was or where he'd come from, I had no idea. It was enough that he was there and cared. The tears started, and a lump in my throat threatened to get the best of me. Roughly, I wiped my sleeve across my torn face, where salty tears stung in the open wounds.

Propped up as I was, a pain in my left shoulder was suddenly almost unbearable, and then I remembered! The gun! My own revolver! I'd been shot at point-blank range. Seating myself, I explored cautiously with my finger. The wound was high, in the juncture of neck and shoulder, and the slug had gone through. It had bled clean and should heal itself.

"C'mere, boy," I commanded. He was sitting now, wondering, I guessed, what this strange human would do next.

I watched his eyes light up; he dropped to his belly, then began to wriggle toward me, his tail wagging joyously. Afraid to take my hands from the ground, I talked to him.

"Good boy," I told him. "Dunno where you come from, feller, but I sure 'preciate you bein' here. Now, you 'n' me are goin' down to thet crick and git us a drink. You jest foller along and keep me comp'ny. Don't you worry none if it takes me a while. I'm gittin' stronger every minute."

The creek was no more than sixty feet from me, but it was a long sixty feet. By that time, I realized that all I had on was my underwear. Them devils had even taken my clothes. Everything was gone! The wagon and team, along with what it contained, plus my saddle horse and pack mule. All of the camp gear, most of it new, that I'd bought with cash money.

It was slow going. I could feel every small pebble on the ground digging into my palms and knees as I crawled to the stream. Halfway there, I fell face down and the dog dashed back to see what was wrong.

"It's okay, boy," I told him. "Jest gimme a break. Sure ain't the man I used to be." I started to laugh—giggle is a better word, I guess—but it hurt so bad, I had to stop.

I shrugged, but that hurt, too. "Sure glad there ain't none of the boys here to see this. Look at me. Tore up like some old range bull! Crawlin' along—" My voice broke; a flood of tears washed down my cheeks, and I pillowed my head on my arms, unable to stop the crying.

Old Dog, he sure was worried. Came over and nuzzled me, whining for me to get up. When that failed, he sat back and howled until it echoed up and down the canyon.

Get up, I berated myself. C'mon! Act like a man! Ain't the first time you got yourself banged up. Think back. Remember the time that old mossyhorn steer cornered you in the brush? Hell, by the time he got done poking and prodding at you, not even your own mother would have recognized you. That wagon boss saved your bacon. Took you into town and got the doc sobered up long enough to put on a few patches. Now, if that don't prove you were born to hang, I'm a muley cow.

Rearing up, madder'n hell, I glared around and started a

crawl for the creek, scuttling like a big crab. Hurting all over, I blotted out the pain and concentrated on getting to the water. Dog ran alongside, barking and growling; he was anxious for my safety and no doubt was wondering why I didn't walk.

In moments I was at the creek's edge, and I plunged headfirst into the shallow water, arms outstretched. For a long while I just lay there, letting the warm water bathe my upper body and gulping thirstily at the surface. There was a noticeable current, and I opened my eyes, watching bits of wood, sticks, and leaves flow past and go downstream. Lazily, I let my body bob up and down, feeling that this was one thing I'd like to do forever. I watched across the creek as a big black stinkbug raised high on his back legs, pushing his pointed head into the mud. I wondered what he would find. I wondered what a stinkbug ate. I wondered what me 'n' the dog were going to eat since all my grub was gone.

The sun was climbing higher, and I could feel the warmth. It was time to try! Somehow, I had to get on my feet, or it was a cinch I'd never live through this fix I was in.

I picked out a gnarled juniper, because it had some thick branches sprouted close to the ground. Perfect for my purpose, because I could use it like a ladder.

Clutching a branch tightly, I gathered my legs under me and painfully pulled myself up, hand over hand on the limbs, until I was erect. Whew! I was weak as a cat. I stood for a time, figuring out what to do next. Now that I was on my feet, what should I do? It had seemed so necessary to be up, and now I didn't know where to begin.

I glanced up at the sun, and estimated it to be about ten o'clock or so. This time of the year, it would stay light until maybe eight o'clock or even later, so I had hours before the sun went down. When it did, it would get cold, and I wasn't exactly dressed for that. Wait a minute . . .

My axe . . . my hand axe. When I'd made my camp, I'd chopped some kindling to get the fire started, and I'd left the axe sunk into the top of an old stump. Maybe they had missed finding it. After all, what reason would they have for a search of the brush? Everything had been out in the open.

"C'mon with me, boy. We're gonna do some lookin'." As I moved off to where I remembered leaving the axe, I hung on to tree limbs as much as I could, and that helped. I had a heck of a lot of things to do and wasn't sure where to begin. A shelter for the night had to be built, but first of all I'd have to clean out my wounds and bind them somehow. The dog and I had to find food, but where? Must be some rabbits running through the brush, but how to catch them? I wondered whether there were fish in the creek. We'd have to look, then rig a line somehow. A trap! I could make a fish trap, a woven fish trap like I'd seen used in Old Mexico. Once the axe was recovered, I could do a lot of things. Peeled bark or maybe some of the vines wound around the trees; both were fine for weaving basket traps. I'd seen deadfalls used for trapping game, but doubted I could lift a log big enough to do the job.

Potatoes! I'd taken my last four potatoes and put them under the coals of my fire last night. By now they had to be cooked just right. Soft and mealy. No! First, I had to find my axe. The potatoes would keep. Besides, I'd have to ration them until I found more food.

The dog was sniffing at every hole in the ground like he knew what he was doing. He looked to be in good shape, so I figured he hadn't been going hungry. Was he really a stray, or did he have a home close by? Suddenly I got very excited, thinking maybe there was a ranch or a miner's cabin not too far away. If so, then he wouldn't hang around past suppertime. Up to now he'd been real friendly, but I'd have bet a silver peso he wouldn't stay with me once his belly started growling. Hopefully, I'd be able to track him if he left.

We found the axe right where I'd left it, and somehow it made me feel better to be armed. It was plenty sharp, and I kept it that way for obvious reasons. I'd sawed the handle off short, so I could carry it more easily, and it looked a lot like an oversized tomahawk.

That got me to thinking about Indians. That'd be about the last straw. Right then I couldn't have fought my way out of a grain sack, and I sure couldn't have taken on a passel of Indians! Back in Santa Fe, they had told me to be careful. Said to be

on the lookout for Mimbres Apaches, because they'd jumped
their reservation and headed for their old hunting grounds. That
was right here, where I was right now. I'd be easy meat. A
good word, that! Meat! Boy, if I just had me a big steak right
now! Hell, forget the meat and forget them Indians. You got
yourself enough to worry about.

My broken finger was giving me fits, so I decided to make a
splint of some kind. It was the longest finger on my left hand,
not the trigger finger. I pulled the left sleeve down, out beyond
my hand, then laid it on the stump and carefully cut off a narrow strip of cloth, then another.

Using the one hand, I split some shavings from the stump and
trimmed them to shape. Carefully, I pulled on the finger until it
reasonably straight. It hurt some, but not enough to make me
holler. I already hurt all over, and one more pain didn't seem to
matter.

Once I'd gotten the finger straightened, I laid a shaving along
eash side and bound them tightly with the cloth. It would have
to be rewrapped as the swelling went down, but I already knew
about such things. I'd managed to break lots of bones in my
twenty-two years, and splints were not a new experience for
this cowhand That got me to brooding. It promised to be a long
time before I'd be in any shape to travel. Even then, I would be
forced to walk, since them coyotes had my wagon and my saddle horse. Tracks wear thin, and this time of year we might
even expect rain. The only one I'd seen was the heavily bearded
man with the gold tooth, and nobody else. I didn't even know
what that other feller *looked* like. Seemed sort of hopeless, but I
wasn't a man to leave things undone. I'd catch up to them two if
it taken the rest of my life! The face of the bearded man came to
mind, vicious and cruel, laughing as he slashed down at my
head with the iron chain. My hands clenched and opened up,
then clenched again in spite of the broken finger. The anger
built in me until I was trembling all over. No matter what it took
to get it done, I'd pay them back in kind.

Bad enough to steal a man's horse! In the Western lands it
was usually a hanging offense, and rightly so. Leaving a man
on foot in a hostile country could mean his death. If Indians

didn't get him the ruggedness of the land itself could kill him. In my case, it was worse. Creeping up in the night and beating me half to death, and for what? A wagon and its load, three horses, a mule and my personal gear? I'd never harmed them, never even *knew* them! They hadn't any call to treat me like this. Trying their best to kill me, and in cold blood! The more I remembered, the madder I got, until I was shaking, in a rage like I'd never before known. I could feel my heart pumping faster and faster, until it threatened to choke me. Must calm myself!

If they'd come into my camp, I would have shared my grub and helped them all I could. It was the custom, and I would expect the same if I was in their boots. No! Instead, the devils had left me for dead or abandoned me, thinking I had little time left. I'd have time, lots of time, to think and plan. Hanging was too good for them two! They would die, but they'd suffer, like I was suffering now. I'd listen to their screams and they'd *beg* to die! I'd show them!

Huh! You *talk* a pretty good fight, cowboy. Chances are, you ain't never gonna see them two again. Let's face it, a couple like them could cross the border. Go down into Old Mexico, where you'll *never* find them. Right now, you'd best worry about getting something to eat and building some sort of shelter so you won't freeze to death.

The dog was just sitting there, staring up at me like he wondered what we were going to do next. So I figured I had best keep him busy, or he might just wander off. The Indian women used dogs for packing light loads, and there wasn't no reason why he couldn't help me. I'd need a collar or something like it to tie on to. The lower strip of my underwear top would work just fine. It was double-hemmed and strong. If I kept cutting up my underwear, I would soon be as naked as a jaybird, and then what would I do? I chuckled.

Tugging my undershirt free, I stretched it taut. Cutting very carefully, I wound up with a two-inch strip about thirty inches long. Next, I cut me a couple of long, sturdy branches and trimmed them. These would be the shafts for a travois, which is a litter sort of arrangement used by Indians that drags behind an animal. The dog stood patiently while I tied the upper ends securely, leaving some slack so that most of the strain would be against his shoulders and not his neck.

Now, bear in mind, I wasn't doing all this handily. "Slow" would be a better word. Just to bend over made sweat break out all over me, and it hurt like hell! I'd been darn lucky not to have broken any more bones. The way that feller had made that chain pop, it's a wonder some of my ribs hadn't busted. Mostly I was just cut up and bruised, and that would heal, given enough time. I'd worked *hard* most of my life, and a feller'd have to hunt some to find any spare fat on me. A bit taller than the average, I stood around five-ten but never weighed more'n 160. Most of my height was in my upper body, and the spread of my shoulders made my arms look extra long.

I reckon that beating would have killed me for sure if I had been a store clerk or worked in a bank. Long hours on a horse, and not always one that was friendly, flanking great big calves so's they could be branded, digging postholes in hard ground until I felt more prairie dog than man! These things had all built slabs of muscle, and that's what saved me from an early grave. I was hurt, all right, but I'd live long enough to see them both dead, and that's what counted.

Once I'd gotten the poles placed and laced in a spreader at the bottom end, I started cutting branches for a lean-to. Actually, what I had in mind was a windbreak, something that would reflect my fire and keep me halfway warm. On top of that load I piled some dry limbs and a few thicker pieces to keep the fire going. Old Dog, he just stood there, not a muscle moving, until I had it all in place.

"C'mon, old feller," I told him. "Let's jest see if this outfit will hold together." With me bent down, holding on to the dog with one hand and leaning on my axe with the other, we moved across to the far side of the clearing.

Once I had sat down, my head quit spinning, and I started plaiting the thinner branches together into a flat rectangle about four feet by six feet, which was enough to give both me and my pal shelter. Then, sharpening one end of a pair of thick stubs, I drove them into the ground with the axe and leaned my new windbreak against them at an angle, just high enough so there'd be room underneath for me and the dog. Now, all that remained was to tie it all together, and for that I had to have some kind of line or lashings.

At first I considered cutting more strips from my underwear, but then I decided to try using soft green bark from a willow. I'd seen a few growing next to the creek. I was a little reluctant to break up my travois, not knowing whether I might find another use for it. My new friend was a strong animal and good-sized. If push came to shove, he might not mind dragging me on the travois, at least for a few miles.

Together, we made it down to the creek bank, and I skinned enough bark to fill my needs without ringing the tree, a caution I hoped would save it. Man is mostly careless when he's living off of nature, but I always figured to leave a little for the next feller.

Back at the fire, I lost no time tying the shelter together. Me 'n' the dog crawled in under it, and I poked about the embers, uncovering my four potatoes. In spite of all my pain, the pangs of hunger were gnawing at my belly, and when I picked up the charred potatoes, I couldn't help myself. A moment later, two had disappeared, skins and all! The third lasted a bit longer, and I fed the skin to the dog. The remaining potato I cached in a corner of the lean-to, but for obvious reasons I wasn't able to forget it.

We lay there for some time, Dog licking his lips and using his front paws to wipe off his whiskers. I pictured the hot steam rising from the potatoes I'd already devoured. With my tongue, I reached around in my mouth, finding a tiny morsel, which I nibbled and savored before I let it slip down my throat. Chances were, the one remaining potato wouldn't taste nearly as good cold, or so I reasoned.

What the heck. One measly potato wasn't going to make a meal. Might as well eat it now, before it cooled. Reaching back, I broke it open and stuffed the hot, moist innards in my mouth, then offered the skin for the dog's reward. Forcing myself to chew slowly, I swallowed and grinned at Dog.

"Well, old horse. Look's like we're gonna have to forage for our next meal. Don't you fret yourself none. I'll git us a rabbit or mebbe a mess of fish. We ain't gonna starve to death. You jest depend on old Jake."

First I built up the fire, using some of the small twigs I'd gathered. On them I put a couple of larger chunks, big enough to keep the fire buning steadily. I was starting to stiffen from by beating, and even a slight movement was a chore. Bathing the wounds with hot water would have helped, but I had no pot to boil it in. I tried to remember some of the remedies I'd seen used. There were roots, leaves, even some flower petals that had healing powers, but I could not remember a single one. One thing I did remember was a bottle of good whiskey I had cached in the wagon. Again, I cursed the two who had put me in this fix. If I had had that whiskey to drink, I wouldn't have been hurting half so much.

A faint breeze had come up, and the dog stood and sniffed in that direction. Whatever he smelled must have been a familiar scent, because he began to whine, and his tail went a mile a minute. Coming back into the shelter, he took hold of my sleeve in his strong jaws and pulled gently. I had just wiggled into a fairly comfortable position, so I resisted, telling him to settle down.

"Easy boy," I told him. "Whatever it is out there will keep for a while. Right now, I'm gonna try and git myself a little shut-eye. How's about laying down here with me just for a couple of hours. Then I'll be fresh as a new-flowered daisy, and we'll go scouting for whatever it is you smell on the wind." As I spoke, my words were already slurring, a sign I might just drop off any minute. Sensing this, Dog replied by doing just as I had asked.

As I was lying on my side with my knees drawn up, he was able to curl up close, with his chin on my outstretched arm. His body was warm, and gratefully I cuddled even closer, a reminder of the days gone by, when I was a youngster and my own pooch used to do the same thing.

CHAPTER 3

I WOKE WITH A START, BURNING WITH FEVER AND soaked in sweat. The fire had died down to a few glowing embers, and the dog had disappeared. I was all alone!

Teeth chattering, I managed to throw on a few twigs, then a pair of larger pieces—enough to get it going again. The sun was low on the horizon, and the day was almost gone. It would soon be dark, and I'd gotten nothing done. Not a bite to eat, and not much chance of finding food in the night.

Pursing my lips, I tried to whistle up the dog, but not a sound came out. "Dog," I called. "Where are you, boy? Sure need you, feller, so c'mon, now!" My voice was so weakened that it scared me, and the thought of being alone scared me more!

Then I heard his paws padding in the dry grass and knew he hadn't abandoned me. A moment later, he poked his moist, inquiring nose under the lean-to and sniffed, bits of furry rabbit hair clinging to his snout. His teeth were bloodied, and he seemed well satisfied with himself.

Before I could speak my piece, he barked and sat back on his haunches, forepaws raised and held together. Sure that he had caught a rabbit and eaten the whole thing, I started cussing him out.

Bewildered, he sat for a moment, studying me with his big eyes, then whining as my tirade continued. When he attempted to lick my hand, I snatched it out of his reach.

"Go on," I bawled. "Git on outta here, you selfish mutt! You ain't my friend. You're nothin' but a pot-lickin' hog. You'd better git before I give you somethin' to really make you cry, you damn, greedy sonofabitch!" I raised my hand.

Still whining, he slunk out of the lean-to, his tail held low. I wanted to call him back. The last thing I wanted to see happen was for him to leave me alone. But stubborn as a sick mule, I bit my lip and kept silent. I'd get along a lot better, I told myself, without some dumb dog to slow me down. This way, I'd only have to worry about feeding my own self, and I'd get by just fine. Good riddance! He wasn't a whole lot of help, anyway.

A minute later, he poked his nose inside and laid a big fresh-killed rabbit on the ground. Reproachfully, he stared for a moment, then turned and left the shelter.

"Wait," I hollered. "Come back, boy! I was only funnin' with you. C'mon, boy! Don't leave poor old Jake here all by his loneself. I'm sorry, Dog! I didn't mean a damn word of what I said; honest, I didn't." I struggled to get up on my knees so I could crawl outside and stop the dog before he left the camp. I didn't have to worry, as it turned out.

There he was, wiggling his whole backside in a frenzy of happiness. He licked my face and pushed me to the ground.

"Hey," I cried out. "Take it easy, feller. I ain't able to take a whole lot of thet!" I was laughing and crying at the same time. I was so darn glad to see him back. Hugging him tightly, I told him how sorry I was for doubting him.

"You 'n' me are sidekicks, old feller. Don't you pay me no mind when I git to spoutin' all thet nonsense. I ain't had no special friend like you before, and I gotta git used to it. C'mon, now! Let's see what we can do with this rabbit before it goes bad on us."

Using my axe blade, I slit the skin on the belly and then turned it inside out. The dog had grabbed it by the back of the neck and had bitten down, so the meat wasn't bloodshot. Using a finger, I got rid of the entrails, and then I spitted the carcass on a green stick. Thrusting the butt end into the ground, I suspended it over the coals.

"It ain't gonna take very long, feller. Hungry as I am, I'll settle for bein' warm." I noticed he was ignoring a chance at the rabbit's innards, so I scooped them up with a leaf and tossed them outside. All the while, I was petting him with my free hand and letting him know I cared.

We sat there waiting, me with my back against one of the posts, staring greedily at the slender carcass impaled on the stick. Slowly it began to turn brown, and the delicious aroma of broiling meat brought saliva to my mouth and caused my belly to rumble. Mentally, I was planning how I would divide our meal. A full half should go to the dog; after all, he *had* provided the rabbit.

But then again, I'd been hurt and had this fever, while he was in real good shape. I really needed solid food more than the dog did. Maybe he'd be satisfied with just a forequarter or perhaps even the back. All dogs liked bones.

No, I'd split it right down the middle. I'd already assured my new friend that we were sidekicks, and so everything had to be divided equally, share and share alike. This brought to mind a conversation I'd had some years back with another good friend.

This feller, Dave Woffard, had said that true friendship must be measured by a willingness to share and to go beyond just being fair. Let's say you've got two steaks over your fire, and one is obviously much better than the other. A real pal would honestly want his buddy to have the choicer cut of the two. Wouldn't just *say* he did but would really mean it, in every way. That, Dave had told me, is real proof of friendship. I chuckled and rubbed the dog's head. It sure beats all, what two cowpokes can find to talk about when they're cooped up in an old line shack and snowed in for the winter.

"Don't you worry none, old feller," I told the dog. "The rabbit's half yours, and you can b'lieve that. I jest wish we had two rabbits, 'cause that'd make it lots easier."

He raised his big head up and stared at me, then whined and

wagged his tail. Hell! I'd oughta be ashamed of thinking thoughts like that. What was wrong with me? I shivered as another chill chased its way down my spine. Putting a hand to my forehead, I found it hot and damp. I needed a doctor or somebody who knew about plants and herbs. At the rate I was going, I'd never leave the clearing, leastways not alive. I shook my head, trying to clear the mists that threatened to creep in, and another chill convulsed my whole body. I shook so violently, my teeth chattered together.

Maybe the rabbit was done and maybe it wasn't, but I had to do something to fight off the sick feeling. I grabbed a handful of grass and slid the rabbit off the stick. It was hot and slick with grease, and I nearly dropped it. My axe blade chopped through the tiny bones, and I split it lengthwise, laying half on the ground in front of the dog.

"Better let it cool off a mite," I warned him. "It might burn your tongue if you're not careful." Ignoring my own warning, I pulled off the hind leg and crammed it in my mouth.

It was hot, all right, but it sure did taste good! Rich and tender. I allowed it was about the best rabbit I'd ever tasted. Greedily, I nibbled away at the meat and sucked at the bones. The dog had better manners and took the advice I'd given him. He watched me gravely as I wolfed down the tiny meal; then I belched and leaned back against the post.

"Go ahead," I told him. "Eat it up, boy! It's cooled by now. Man, what I wouldn't give for a smoke right now! It might kill me, but I'd sure as heck die happy." I closed my eyes and listened as the dog crunched his portion in powerful jaws. I felt sleepy and somewhat warmer now. Might just catch me a few winks, I thought to myself. It probably would do me some good. Besides, it was dark out there, and I couldn't do much of anything if I couldn't see.

Reaching over, I added some wood to my fire, enough so it would burn for a couple of hours at least. My shoulder was really giving me fits where the bullet had punched through, and my whole right side was paining me considerably. There really wasn't anything I could do except try to keep my arm from moving about and favor it all I possibly could. Washing it in the creek water seemed to help, but I wasn't sure if that was the right thing to do. I'd wait until daylight, and if it showed signs of inflammation, I'd have to cauterize it with fire. That prospect wasn't a happy one.

Lying down under the shelter, I scrunched around until I felt halfway comfortable, and then I closed my eyes. A moment later, I felt the warm comfort of the dog's body as he snuggled in against me, yawned a big, wide one, and muttered some sort of moaning, grunting sound. A deep breath, one seeming to go on forever, then a gradual relaxing as he emptied his lungs and lay still. His breathing was very shallow, as if he didn't want to disturb me.

I lay awake for a while. It wasn't just the pain but more a wonderment at what was happening now. Last night, it had been much the same. I'd finished my supper, scoured the frying pan with sand, and rinsed it in the creek, along with my plate and cup, then spread out my bedroll and turned in. Tired after a long day, I'd dropped off to sleep just as I closed my eyes. I'd awakened, of course, to the pain of the beating that had almost killed me. Given any kind of deal, I would have laid odds against my chances of surviving.

Now, I ain't exactly a churchgoing man. Sure, my folks read the Bible on Sundays, and whenever a circuit rider came around, they'd haul me off to town, and I'd be forced to pay attention to what he had to say. Many was the times my paw or my maw would have to poke me in the ribs because I dropped off to sleep during the sermon. I knew there was a God up there somewhere, but I'd never studied on it much, just sorta took it for granted, I guess.

Far as praying goes. I hadn't done much of that since I'd run off and turned my hand to working cattle. I ain't saying I hadn't never hollered something like "God help me" when I was in some kind of trouble, mebbe up to my chin in a bog or trying to outrun a herd of stampeding longhorns over the worst durn country you ever did see. No! Like many a man before me, I called on somebody up there when there weren't nobody else to turn to. That's natural, I guess, and yet He ain't never let me down.

Take now, for instance. There I was, all busted up, and not a soul around to give me a hand. Then along happens my new friend, the dog. Not only does he help me out, but he's there to cheer me up and let me know he cares. Next thing, he goes out and fetches in a big rabbit for our supper. Now that's a whole saddlebag full of coincidences, ain't it! It makes a man wonder, if nothing else.

CHAPTER 4

I DOZED IN FITS AND SNATCHES THAT NIGHT, TWIST-ing, turning, half delirious with pain and fever. When the sky began to lighten in the east, I knew that I had to do something to better my condition or I just plain wasn't going to make it through the day. Before long I'd be too weak even to raise a hand to help myself. Then I would die.

The wound in my shoulder hurt something fierce, like some jagged lance was probing at it, and my whole body was aching with pain. Shuddering with a chill and burning with fever, I reached out toward the nearly dead fire and took hold of one of the branches. The end still glowed dully and might be coaxed into flame. Gently at first, I blew on the faint coal until it turned orange, then harder until it whitened with heat. About as big around as my wrist, it would do the trick if I had the guts to try it.

Loosening my undershirt, I pulled it away from the wound; then, teeth clenched, I jammed the burning brand against the reddened bullet wound. Smoke billowed up in my face, and my mouth came open as I screamed in anguish and fell backward against the dog's shaggy side.

Strangely enough, I remained conscious, but my belly felt knotted, and the bile rose in my throat. The dog whined and wriggled out from under me, then sat there, his eyes staring at me in wonder. Slowly, things came back into focus, and I was able to sit up. I grinned wryly. "Well, partner," I told him, "we got the easy part done. Now, let's try again. Too bad you can't help, 'cause reachin' around is gonna be a real chore!"

Cautiously, I brought my right hand around and found the hole where the ball had gone through. Though a bit ragged, it wasn't as bad as I had feared. Had it hit the bone, the bullet would have flattened out, and I would've had lots more to worry about. Picking up a clean stick, I practiced reaching around back of my neck and touching the wound until I felt I could to it every time.

Once more, I blew on the end of my brand until it showed white. Then, steeling myself, I reached around and touched it to the wound. This time I didn't make a sound, but that wasn't because I didn't want to. The stink of burning flesh filled the lean-to, and everything spun around for a moment. My throat was dry, and my shoulder hurt like hell! Time for another trip to the creek. I could almost taste the water's cool freshness. Suddenly I felt strange, and it was like a cloud had come down over my eyes. Everything was black again, a terrifying blackness that whirled me off to a place where I could hear a voice crying something but couldn't make out the words. It was cold. Bitter cold! I was spinning above a deep canyon, and I could feel hands trying to drag me down to the bottom. I fought back, but I was so weak that I couldn't make them let go of me.

Then it was daylight. A bright sun was shining, and the dog had my sleeve in his jaws. Whining, he pulled at me in an attempt to get me moving again. Or at least it seemed that was what he had in mind.

I sat up, and for a moment everything whirled around. My head ached badly, and my face felt hot. I knew I'd never be able to make it down to the creek, but I would have to think of something, and soon! The travois! If I could get him in the harness and somehow tie myself on the contraption, maybe the dog could find us some help somewhere.

On my knees, I crawled out of the lean-to and over close to the makeshift rig. Picking up the cloth bands, I called: "C'mere, boy! C'mon, I gotta git this on you, and pretty darn quick, before I pass out again."

Obediently, he came and positioned himself between those two poles I'd rigged. After considerable fumbling, I managed to tie the harness around his neck. Then came the hardest task, securing my carcass to the travois. My undershirt would have to go, or at least a good portion of it. I couldn't think of anything else to use.

With some difficulty, I contrived to get it off, but I paid for the effort with considerable pain. Using the axe, I cut off both sleeves and split each into two strips. Gingerly, I was able to get what was left of it back on and buttoned.

Just plain thinking was a chore, but I figgered out a way to do the job. First, I got myself into a sitting position on the frame. Then, spreading my legs, I tied each thigh to one of the poles. The axe had come in mighty handy; you can bet on that! Without it, we'd have been out of luck. So I made a loop in the tie on my right leg and slipped the handle in there. It hung easy and close to my hand.

Like I said earlier, my arms were overlong for my height, so each strip was about three feet long. Tying two of them together, I passed that length around my chest in a complete circle, with the two ends crossing at my breastbone. Then I tied them to the poles as tightly as I could, using doubled wraps so they couldn't slip down.

Mind you, I didn't get all of this done at once. Twice I must have passed out momentarily, and each time it taken me a few minutes to remember what I had in mind to do. If that creek had been a mite closer, it would have helped. Splashing some of that cold water in my face sure would have felt good! Right about then, I could have used a nice long drink, too, but I had to stop thinking about that.

Then came the hardest part of all, making the dog understand what I needed him to do. I shook my head and heaved a big sigh. Whatever was in my head that would make me believe the dog would carry me anywhere? I was doing all this by guess and by golly, with no real plan. It was no more than the wild dreams of a sick man who had no alternatives. Hell! I could probably consider myself lucky if the animal didn't drag me all over a couple of hundred acres just trying to free himself. But I had to try something.

Craning my neck, I spoke to him softly. "Go home, old feller. Home, boy! We can't just stand around here. Head for home, wherever that is. C'mon, boy! *Vaya!*" I used one of the Mexican words for "go," thinking maybe he'd know that one better'n plain old American.

For a long moment he just stood there. Then, grunting a bit with the effort, he started to move out. He was a fine, big dog, weighing more'n a hundred pounds and lots stronger than most. Once we got to moving, it seemed to be no effort for him, and we were on our way. Where? I had no idea, but I figured sooner or later we'd come upon some folks who'd help me. I'd seen fresh cow and horse droppings all through the canyon, and there had to be men taking care of them.

I wasn't feeling all that good about then. The shoulder wound had partially scabbed over, but wrestling with the undershirt and crawling around had broken it open, and it had begun bleeding again. I remembered seeing the Indians with those contraptions, and they had always had a pile of buffalo or deer hides cushioning the ride. I cussed the fact that I'd left the rabbit skin behind. I could have used it to pad my wounded shoulder. Right now that shoulder was giving me fits, rubbing against the bark on the pole, hurting enough that I tensed my belly muscles and tried to twist away. Trouble was the dragging pole ends would drop into a chuckhole and throw me back against it, and I'd have to holler. Finally, I reached around with my left hand and held it behind my back. It was not the best cure, but it helped keep the wound from rubbing against the rough bark.

Seemed like we'd been on the move for hours, when suddenlike the dog stopped and whined. I twisted my head around and watched him sniffing the air, like maybe he could tell someone was close by. Or something! Be my luck to run into one of them Mexican pumas. Bigger than the cougars you

find farther north, these critters weren't so apt to back off. I had
seen one killed a couple years back, and he'd have made a pair
of the regular varieties. Might even be a pack of them javelinas,
the fierce little wild pigs that roamed those mountains. A man
on foot stood a good chance of getting bad hurt by them. Their
tusks were sharp, and they could tear a man's legs to ribbons.
Ferocious little beasts, they had to be mortally hit, and with a
large-caliber ball, before you'd stand a chance. There I was,
flat on my back, helpless, easy prey for them nasty critters!

We were stopped on what appeared to be a game trail running
through a thicket of juniper and pinyon. Only a glimpse of blue
sky could be seen through the interlaced branches of the trees
overhead, and there was a thick tangle of brush on both sides. I
doubted a man could have stood upright, as the path obviously
had been made by animals.

There was some rustling on my right, and I craned my neck
around, staring straight into the bore of a rifle. The hole looked
big enough to chamber a peach, or at least that was how it appeared to me at the time. The dog was whining, frisking about
with his tail going a mile a minute. Then he let go with a deep,
sonorous bark and tried his best to get rid of the travois. There
wasn't all that much room on the game trail, but he still managed to tip me over as the poles got tangled and one twisted free
of the makeshift harness.

Pain shot through my shoulder as I rolled over. My face
smacked into the ground, and my mouth filled with leaves and
dirt. I was about as helpless as a man can get, tied tightly to the
travois poles with one arm twisted behind my back.

I could hear the thrashing of tree branches, and I sensed the
presence of someone standing close by. With an effort, I
twisted my head to one side and saw a pair of bronzed legs en-
cased in knee-length moccasins and the edge of a deerskin skirt.
The yawning muzzle of a Winchester carbine hung next to the
hem, with two eagle feathers dangling near the sight. Before I
had a chance to do or say anything, that durn old blackness
closed in, and I was off again, whirling around in ever-
widening circles over that deep canyon, with cold winds chill-
ing me to the bone.

CHAPTER 5

∞∞∞∞∞∞∞∞∞∞∞∞∞∞∞∞∞∞∞∞∞∞∞∞∞∞∞∞∞∞∞∞

How long I was unconscious, I couldn't say, not for sure! I sorta remember something cool on my head and the soothing touch of gentle hands. But I ain't ever going to forget my terror of that blackness and that deep canyon, because they showed up many times while I was trying to come back to the real world—the one without bitter cold and burning heat.

Then suddenly I was awake, and I heard the welcome whine of the dog. Heard a quail sounding his warning notes. Felt a cool breeze on my face. Smelled meat roasting and knew I was going to be all right. Knew I wouldn't die; not now!

For a long moment I kept my eyes closed, not sure what I might see but mighty darned glad just to be alive. I still hurt all over, but the fever seemed to be gone, and my head didn't ache like before. My left arm lay on my chest, and my shoulder appeared to be bound in some kind of bandage.

Feeling around with my good hand, I decided I was on some sort of deerskin pallet, with grasses or willow boughs under the hides. It was soft and mighty comfortable. Moving the hand must have caught somebody's eye, because I heard sounds of footsteps crunching in gravel and heading my way. Still keeping my eyes tightly closed, I waited.

The footsteps stopped by my side, and I sensed the warmth of someone bending close, caught the grass-sweet scent of an exhaled breath, heard the rustle of clothing as a hand felt my forehead. I opened my eyes and gazed into a pair of the prettiest brown orbs you ever did see. Shaded by long and silky black lashes under a lightly bronzed brow, they looked me over with frowning concern. My rescuer, or my captor, was an Indian girl, and a mighty pretty one to boot!

"Well," she said, "I see you've decided to wake up. I've some warm broth here, and I want you to try and sit up so I can get it into you." She reached out. "Here! Take hold of my hand, and I'll help you."

Perplexed, I just lay there for a moment and stared. I guess that was mostly because she appeared to be Indian, and yet her English was better'n mine. Also, I was still trying to figure out where I was and how I'd gotten there. She was really a beautiful girl! "Woman" was a better word, because I couldn't help noticing she was well filled out. Not plump, you understand, more like buxom. Though she was tall and slender in build, her worn doeskin dress was taut across a full bosom.

Up close, I could see the delicate bones in her face and a narrow, aristocratic nose that sure didn't fit any Indian I'd ever seen. Her hair shone blue-black in the sunlight, a perfect match for heavy, arched brows that contrasted vividly with her creamy, tanned skin. Her full mouth, pursed in a frown, spread in a slight smile as she sensed my perplexity.

"You wonder how I am able to speak your language so well? Be patient, and I'll explain later. Right now, it's important that you drink this broth. It will give you strength."

I taken hold of her hand and felt the strong grip and a callused palm. With a heave, she helped me sit up. Meat broth ain't much of a meal for a growed man, but I was purely glad to get most anything right then. I felt the warmth all the way down and felt better almost immediately. Handing back the empty bowl, I looked up at her questioningly.

She nodded, her face expressionless. "We have more," she

said. "I'll bring you another bowl, and then we'll give you something more solid to eat. It isn't wise to hurry things, until your stomach has had a chance to settle down. Stay as you are, and I'll be right back with the broth."

I watched as she turned and walked toward the fire, an uneasy feeling in my mind. Something was wrong here, and I couldn't put my finger on it. She was sure enough trying to help me, but it seemed like she was doing it reluctantly. I could understand in a way, because after all, there wasn't a lot of love lost between Indians and whites. But this was more than just that. Besides, what was a lone Indian girl doing way out there in the wilderness? Where were her folks hiding out? Was this some kind of ritual camp, and was I in the way, so to speak? Maybe she'd done something wrong and the tribe had driven her out, forced her to forage for herself until she proved she could do it.

I watched her bend over a pot and ladle some more of the broth into the bowl. She straightened and started back toward me. All of a sudden, something landed right behind my back with a thump and let out a shriek so loud that it almost busted my eardrums! I like to jump out of my skin, and I twisted around so fast that I lost my balance and fell flat.

Spitting dirt out of my mouth, I peered up at the skinny old Indian man who stood over me with my hatchet held high over his head. The skin was stetched so tightly on his face that it seemed more like a skull. Adding to the illusion, a circle of black paint ran around each of his eyes, and a dab of the same was under his cheekbones. A broad band of white covered his mouth and jaw, with spots of red speckling here and there like drops of blood. He screamed again and did a sort of dance, brandishing the hatchet and gobbling something to me in Apache. Right away I could tell he was not exactly happy about me being there.

The girl hollered something at him, but he didn't pay her no mind, continuing to prance up and down as he rasped some sort of gibberish at me. Finally, she got in close and was able to calm him down. Even then, I wasn't sure but what I had little time left to live. That old man was really mad!

She reached out and taken the hatchet out of his hand, a lucky thing for me, because I figured he was about to use it to part my scalp permanently. He quieted down and shuffled away, but not without giving me one last murderous glare.

The girl laid down the hatchet and the bowl and gave me a hand in sitting up again. She didn't offer me any explanation, and I didn't ask for none. One thing for sure; I'd best keep both eyes on that old coot. That is, if I figured to go on breathing. He'd given up for now, but it was plain to see what his feelings were toward me. He wouldn't quit until he had my scalp drying on a willow hoop, and bad hurt like I was, there wasn't much I could do to defend myself.

The second bowl of broth tasted as good as the first, but I was still mighty hungry. When I held out the bowl for the third refill, the girl shook her head. "Not yet," she said. "You must wait for a while. You've been too long without a proper meal, and more will only make you sicker." She turned away, but I called out and asked her to wait a moment.

"How long have I been here?" I asked. "I remember strappin' myself on to thet contraption back by the crick, but not anything more. Did the dog come here, or did you find us?"

"A little bit of both," she replied. "We were tracking a pair of white men who murdered my husband. The dog followed them after I shot one in the shoulder. I don't think he was badly hurt, just a flesh wound. We couldn't leave right away, after all; we had my husband to bury. I was sure that the dog would return when he was certain the men were gone. Why he helped you is a mystery. He never cared for whites.

"After the burial, we began tracking the dog and the two men. It was very easy for us, as they left sign that even a child could follow. When we ran into you, the dog was backtracking his own trail, headed toward our old camp. As for you, you've been unconscious for two days. I helped you, as I would help anyone who was hurt, but once your wounds have healed, you must leave. White men killed my husband! White men drove us from our home! You are just another white man, and no different from those others."

I looked up, startled by what she'd just said and excited by what it could mean. Two white men! Could they be the same coyotes who had bushwhacked me? Maybe my chances were better than I'd thought. Maybe I *could* catch up with them. I didn't miss the bitterness in her voice or misunderstand when she'd talked about whites. Changing her mind would not come easy. Why had I thought about that? Why should I be worrying whether she liked or disliked anybody? Right now that would have to wait. What I needed was information, all that I could get, no matter what. That came first!

"Exactly when did all this happen?" I asked her. "Was it recent-like, say, 'bout five, six days back? You must've gotten a pretty good look at them two. Can you describe them?"

She studied the ground for a moment, then looked up. "It happened so fast, and I was fighting back. The shock. We didn't know anyone was nearby. Wait. Both men were wearing soldier's clothing, or what was left of it. Neither had shoes, and their feet were bleeding. One man was much larger than the other, and he had a beard. The other man needed a shave, but his whiskers weren't long, more like four or five days' growth on his face. It was he who killed my . . ."

It was hurting her to talk about this, but I had to know. Maybe if I could distract her for a while, give her time to collect her thoughts. . . . "Say," I asked, "you ain't got some tobacco around here, have you? I'd 'bout give both eyeteeth for a smoke. Any old kind of a smoke! You gotta have a few questions of your own. I'll tell you most anythin' if you can jest come up with some real tobacco, ma'am."

She smiled, the first real smile I'd seen since waking up in her camp. Turning on her heel, she walked over to a sort of shelter on the far side of the clearing. Bending over, she hunted through a hide packsack, laying things over to one side as she searched. Finally she found what she'd been looking for, replaced all the other stuff, and returned to where I was lying. The smile was no longer there, but in her hand was a pipe and a leather pouch.

"Here," she told me. "This was my husband's. You may use it if you like. That is, if the fact that an Indian had it in his mouth doesn't bother you." The last was said bitterly and with no trace of a smile. No expression at all!

Reaching up, I taken the pipe and pouch from her hand. I knew it was important to say the right thing, but I couldn't quite find the words. Then I decided the truth would be the best and began to talk as I stuffed the pipe with tobacco. I kept my eyes on hers all the while.

"Ma'am," I said, "a man is a man, no matter what the color of his skin. There's good ones and there's bad ones in all of us. I figgered out a long time ago thet I'd judge a man by his actions, by the way he treated other men. What I am tryin' to say, ma'am, is thet we are individuals, each to be respected or despised or even ignored accordin' to how we act around others. Your man was a good one, and I'll bet on thet, 'cause it's easy to see you're a good woman, and it jest don't figger you'd stay long with a man thet wasn't decent and fair. Thet's jest common sense.

"One of the finest men I ever knew was half Injun. Still is, if he's still alive. He was my last boss. Him and his two brothers. Their daddy was a full-blood Choctaw. Now I ain't gonna lie to you and say I ain't never shot me no red Injuns. I have, not once but several times. But they was shootin' at me whilst I was defendin' myself and the cattle thet belonged to my boss." I'd finished loading the pipe.

"Say," I asked her. "Would you mind fetchin' me a burnin' stick outta thet fire there? These things don't work good 'less'n you git 'em lit up." I grinned with the pipe stuck in my teeth. "You got any more questions, ma'am?"

She shook her head and sat there staring at me. Now, my experiences with ladies had been pretty limited. Real ones, I mean. Most nice girls wouldn't have anything to do with a cowpuncher like me, and that's a fact. This one was a real lady, regardless of her color. She got up and went over to the fire, poked around a little bit, and came back with that stick I'd asked for. I thanked her politely and set about getting the pipe going good. By golly! I gotta tell you, a feller don't really appreciate a smoke until he's had none for a spell. I drew on the pipe hard until my lungs hurt, then exhaled and drew in another. Now, that maybe sounds a bit foolish, but it was purely a pleasure to me. Bet on it!

I leaned back and taken another good look at her. Some

women just naturally look fine no matter where they are or what they're wearing. 'Course, like I said, I wasn't used to being around *good* women. I reckon the only one I'd ever had really close to me was my mother, so you see what I mean.

The railhead towns at the end of every cattle drive had a sort of imaginary line that divided the saloons, bathhouses, and bordellos from the homes of the decent folks. A tough marshal was always there to enforce that line and to make sure no evil-minded cow nurse strayed into that forbidden territory. Sure, they made their living off of us: the storekeepers, the blacksmiths, and the rest of the merchants in those towns. But woe betide any cowboy who wandered in them fancy neighborhoods. To them, he was just a dirty, illiterate rover who didn't have the gumption to settle down and make an honest living. So they'd sic that marshal onto the poor feller, and he'd wind up in the jail. Whatever the saloon girls had left in his pockets went into the marshal's poke, and next morning he'd be told to get out of town. I'd had it happen to me, but only once! Man don't have to smack me over the head with a pick handle to show me good sense.

Hell! I try to keep myself as clean as the next man. A feller eats a lot of dust riding drag behind a couple thousand cows, and sometimes there ain't enough water for drinking, much less taking a bath. But when we went into towns, you can be sure we wore our Sunday best, and we were cleaner than most of them slick-talking shopkeepers. Why, some fellers would spend a month's wages on a hat, and maybe two on a pair of boots. When we invested in a suit, it was never a ready-made off the shelf, but custom-tailored. Fancy spurs and solid silver belt buckles could eat up a year's pay, and a good saddle was something to choose carefully.

Of course, once we'd drunk the town dry and finished our shenanigans, we might look like the last rose of summer—sorta wilted. We'd be broke, or at least badly bent, and we knew that that celebration might have to last us another year or so. That's when we'd pull our six-shooters and try to shoot holes in the sky. Now and then, some cowpuncher's aim might be a little bit off, and he'd bust a window or shoot out one of the streetlamps. The marshal'd come a-running, and we'd have to skedaddle or wind up in his jail.

Them's the cowboys the townfolks remember. Not them boys who trail the stock there and justify the town's existence. Not the ones who spend their last dollars in the stores or waste their money in the saloons. Nope! They just remember how much that window cost to replace and how downright disgusting them drunken punchers carried on.

"Are you all right?" The girl's query startled me, and I rubbed an arm across my eyes. Sitting up, I had to wait for a moment before I could give her an answer.

Grinning sheepishly, I held up my hands. "Yes, ma'am, I'm jest fine! Reckon I was sorta daydreamin' about times that've gone by. Part of it's your fault. No! Wait jest a minute. I didn't mean thet like it might sound. It's jest thet you're so darned pretty sittin' there with the sun in your hair, and I let myself git carried away. Couldn't help myself. You see, ma'am, a man who's in my line of work seldom gits chances to be close to a beautiful woman, much less a really nice girl like you who nurses him back to health. Honest, ma'am, you're the most beautiful woman I ever saw!"

Now, a lot of women couldn't have handled something like that. Some would've blushed and turned away. Others might take it for granted and preen themselves like a prairie hen. This one accepted if for just what it was, an honest compliment intended to show my appreciation for what she was and what she was doing for me. She spoke up, her eyes intent on mine and her tones low and purposeful.

"There was one more thing about one of those men that I remember clearly. The bearded man had a gold tooth, and it was very noticeable since the rest of his teeth were broken and blackened by tobacco. He is the one I shot at twice."

I was excited! There was no longer any doubt in my mind. That was the man who had beaten me with the chain! I told her a little about the beating and about seeing that tooth in the moonlight. "It showed up like a new penny," I told her.

"I gotta git healed up, and mighty quick," I went on, the words tumbling out in my excitement. "Thet wagon will make a trail thet a greenhorn could foller. It's loaded up with mining equipment I was supposed to deliver near Lordsburg."

Not thinking, I tried to stand and fell over sideways on the ground. " 'Scuse me, ma'am. Lordy! I ain't got me no sense at all! It's jest thet thinkin' about them two murderin' coyotes gits my dander up, and I lose track of what's goin' on here. I know thet I gotta be patient and wait until I git better, but it jest burns me up rememberin' all I lost to them devils and how hard I worked to git it. Taken every cent I earned goin' up the trail to Abilene for that wagon and the harness. The team was given to me by my old boss, and they were big, heavy horses. My saddle horse and the riggin', my guns and camp gear, even every stitch I owned, plus the clothes on my back. They taken it all!"

Suddenly I realized how my losses compared to hers, and I apologized again. "I'm sure sorry, ma'am! Here I lie hollerin' about what I've lost, and they taken your husband. Killed him dead, and you about to have his child!" Damn! I had done it again. Man wasn't supposed to talk of some such things in front of a woman. I started to apologize for the blunder but stammered so much that I really made it worse.

She actually laughed! Covered her mouth and turned away from me, her shoulders shaking with laughter. Me? I wanted to find a hole in the ground and crawl into it. What a big dummy I'd turned out to be. Pregnancies weren't things you talked about, no matter how obvious they might be. Then she turned around and, still smiling let me off the hook.

"Please don't bother to apologize, Mister . . . We've never gotten around to introductions. What should I call you?" I told her I'd been christened Jacob Bailey, but friends called me Jake, and I'd be real pleased to have her do likewise.

Still red-faced, I asked her name. "That is, if you're of a mind to tell me," I said. "My mother raised me to have manners, but you'd never know it now. Trouble is, I had no reason to remember them. Leastways, not recently."

She nodded and sat down next to my pallet. Reaching for the pipe, which I had laid aside, she began thumbing tobacco into the bowl. "I used to do this for my husband," she told me, "and he said it tasted much better when I did. My name is Na-li-igai, which means 'White Maiden' in your language."

She handed me the pipe and went toward the fire for the light I needed. Returning, she held a burning twig over the bowl until I had it going good. Stamping out the twig with a moccasined foot, she sat down again and continued.

"My grandfather was called Mangas Coloradas, a name given to him by Mexicans. He married with a Mexican captive, even though his people objected. They had four lovely daughters, and one of them became my mother.'

"Grandfather Mangas was a wise man, and he knew that only by banding together could we have any chance against whites and Mexican soldiers. So he married those daughters off to chiefs of the *Shis-Inday*, the name we call ourselves. Maybe 'Apache' is a Mexican word; I'm not sure. To us, we are the People of the Woods, or *Shis-Inday* in our language. One is the wife of Cochise, a Chiricahua. Another wed Hash-kai-la, of the Coyoteros. The third became the bride of Ku-tu-hala, chief of the White Mountain Apaches. I am the daughter of a lesser chief of the Mimbres, Na-ka-yen, or 'Keen Sighted.'

"My father has some white blood in his veins, a gift from one of his grandfathers, who was a French free trapper. The trappers would rendezvous in Taos and become very drunk, and in their drunken games they would sometimes kill each other.

"When my grandmother was still alive, she used to tell me stories of these hairy, boisterous men, who were really more like the Indians than the Indians themselves. Her father, a chief of the Mimbres, sold her for twenty horses, a rifle, and keg of rum. That was a big bride price, and she acted very proud when she would tell me of this."

She looked down at the ground and sifted some of the red dirt in her hands. "So, you see," she said, looking right square into my eyes, "I am a mixture of many bloods. Not an Indian, nor a white, nor a Mexican! What do you think of me now, white man? What do you think of a woman who can claim no people for her own?" She flung the handful of dirt and stood up, looking down at me from her slim height as I considered what I was about to say. Just the barest bulge made her pregnancy noticeable, and she was so very lovely.

"Ma'am," I replied, "this is gonna sound mighty sudden to you, but I'd give most anything to have you for *my* wife! To answer your question, mixed blood is common with folks. Me, for instance. I'm what we call a Duke's Mixture. My mother is Scotch-Irish, and my daddy was part English, along with a smatterin' of French and German. Hell! He might even had a mite of Injun blood in him, 'cause his family was around the colonies way back in the early days, when women was scarce as hen's teeth. So, you see, I'm sorta like a mongrel, part of many nations. What counts is the individual, like I told you before. I wasn't joshin', ma'am, when I spoke up like I did. You *are* the most beautiful woman I've ever laid these tired eyes on, and I want you for my own. Now! What've you got to say to thet?'' I lay back exhausted and hurting in every part of my body but jubilant about having spoken my piece.

She bent down and fussed over me, adjusting the blanket and brushing the hair back from my face. Then she smiled at me and cocked her head to one side quizzically.

''You speak big words,'' she said, ''for a man who has nothing to offer. Look at you! Not even a pair of pants! Pray tell, Mister Jake Bailey, how do you plan to care for me? I see no horses. You have no rifle, and rum costs money. You cannot even care for yourself, and yet you speak of marrying me. I think it is the fever talking, not you!''

Leaning forward, she kissed me gently on my forehead, a light smoldering in her dark eyes. ''I thank you, Jake. For what you said and how you've made me feel. You are a kindly man, and I am a foolish girl, spouting nonsense. Now you must try to sleep. Rest is what you must have now, because it will help more than any medicine. Your wounds are not so serious as they could be; it's just that there are so many. You've taken a terrible beating, but you're a strong, healthy man, and you are young. The young heal easily.''

I barely heard her last words. Sleep came swiftly, and this time my dreams were happy ones. No more cold winds or deep canyons; instead, I dreamed of grassy meadows way up on the high mesas, where a black-haired girl rode a proud young stallion with a golden mane and tail.

CHAPTER 6

IN SPITE OF ALL MY PAINS, THE NEXT TEN DAYS PASSED by in record time and were some of the happiest I had ever known. At supper the second day, I ate my first solid food since they'd found me. Na-li-igai had shot a good-sized javelina, and it turned out to be a sow. We had hunted through the thickets to uncover her den, which contained a half dozen little ones. I'd eaten almost two of them tender li'l rascals before I could stop, and I went to sleep that night with a full belly.

Once Na-li-igai explained how I had come to be hurt, that ornery old man quit giving me the evil eye. Mind you, I was still a white man as far as he was concerned, and not to be completely trusted no matter the circumstances. He kept as far away from me as he could. At mealtimes he'd grab what food she dished out for him and then squat down over on the far side of the clearing to eat it.

During the daylight hours, I'd watch him climb up a small hill nearby and hunker down. He'd stay up there all day, watching so that nobody could sneak in and surprise us. At midday, she would take him some food and an olla of water. He'd just nod his thanks and keep on sitting up there, with his eyes scanning around. Far as I could see, he had no gun with him, only a long lance with feathers tied on one end.

Near as I can recall, it was maybe the sixth day that he came up behind me and squatted down. Without saying a word to me, he picked up my pipe and taken out one of his own, a short, stubby one with the bowl carved in the likeness of a man's head. Reaching into the folds of his shirt, he fetched a deerskin pouch filled with coarse tobacco. With a great deal of care, he packed both pipes, tamping them with a stub of one scarred thumb; the first joint was completely missing.

Once the pipes were done to his satisfaction, he handed me one and then reached back into his shirt. This time it was an end of antelope horn that he brought out. Holding one finger up to draw my attention, he pried at the butt with his thumb and fore-finger until it came loose, revealing the heads of some wooden matches stored in the cavity.

"Lucifers," he told me with a grin. Scratching the head of one on a rock, he cupped it in his palm and held it over the bowl of my pipe. Once I got it going, he lighted up his own and puffed away with a pleased look on his wrinkled old face as his eyes began to close. After a moment, he opened them a fraction and peered at me through the slits.

Sucking noisily, he drew in a mouthful of smoke and exhaled it slowly, savoring the taste. Reaching forward with his pipe, he tapped me on my arm. "You name Jeke," he said, grinning widely. "You good mans. Soon, you better, an' you fin' bad mans. You, me, we kill bad mans." Then he tapped my arm again and pointed to himself, baring toothless gums in a broad smile and nodding his head in affirmation.

"Long time 'go," he continued, "me name Tset-a-go-hn. It mean I no like no mans, but like fight all mans. You ask it from she." He pointed towards Na-la-igai. "She tell you. Now, me name Hasti ki dn. Too old now, but still wan' fight bad mans. Wan' kill bad mans. Bad mans no dam' good!"

"You, me," he went on, "we frien's." He taken a hold on my good arm and laid his skinny one alongside mine.

"No same color," he said, "but same here!" He tapped his

heart. "We wan' kill bad mans; bad mans kill *mi hijo*." For a moment he looked puzzled, realizing that I couldn't understand. He looked around trying to figure out how to show me.

Then he put both arms across his chest and rocked back and forth like a mother would rock her child. "*Hijo, hijo!* You know, Jeke. *Mi hijo!*"

I suddenly realized that he was trying to say "son," and I nodded to him. "*Hijo*," I repeated. "Son. Your son. They are the men who killed your son!"

Vigorously, he nodded his head in affirmation. "Bad mans kill son. Dja-o-aha son of me. Dja-o-aha hoosban' of she."

After some more of the same talk, he let me know he had a job to do and pointed up to the hill. I nodded and thanked him for the tobacco and the conversation. Later on, I asked Na-li-igai what his two names meant, and she told me.

"Tset-a-go-hn means 'renegade' in our language. He used to be a very brave warrior but a lonely man, and by his own choice. He had no friends and didn't seem to care. He had a wife, and she bore him the one son, Dja-o-aha, but he took her sister also, and they had no children. The two sisters cared for the boy like he belonged to them both. So that's why their son was named as he was. Dja-o-aha means 'Mothers Married to Same Man.' Not all Mimbres men want two wives, a majority being content with just one. Tset-a-go-hn would go from the village without telling anyone where he was going. He was sometimes gone for weeks, until everyone had given up ever seeing him again.

"Then he would return, bringing with him perhaps a dozen horses, many guns, and other war trophies. He never did reveal where he had been or who he had fought with and killed. When I was a little girl, I was afraid of him, like the others were, even the chiefs.

"But something happened to him on one of those lone war trails. He came back to the village on foot and unarmed, with a bad wound in his side and covered with small knife cuts all over his body. He wouldn't tell anyone what had happened to him, but it was whispered that he'd been captured by the Mexican militia and tortured. Somehow he had escaped, but it made him a coward. From that day on, he was afraid of everything and everyone. If it hadn't been for his two wives, who loved him, he would have starved or been driven from the band. They hunted for food, fed him, and protected him from all of the others. Now he is old; his wives are both dead, and no one cares about him. Except, of course, for me.''

"What about thet other name?" I asked. "How'd he come about gittin' thet one? Hasty Kiddin' or something sounding like thet. The way he talked, it don't count for much.''

She smiled. "He is called Hasti-ki-dn, which means 'Old One' in our tongue. This is a recent name. Before, when a number of our people were cruel to him, they taunted him by calling him Hitcadn, meaning 'He Cries.' Even little children made fun of him and threw sticks and stones at him. He never fought back, no matter how badly they treated him.''

Like I said, them ten days was really fine ones. I'd gotten to calling her Nelly, or Nell, because her Indian name was a real tongue twister. She said she didn't mind none, and so she was Nell to me from then on. I'd also taken to calling the old man Pop, and he thought that was all right once I explained what it meant. We spent about an hour every day just sitting there and talking before he went up on top of that hill where he stood guard.

By the end of the first week I could get around about as well as you'd expect. The shoulder was stiff, and I favored it some, but otherwise I was feeling pretty good. Nell was feeding me enough to keep a bunkhouse crew in good shape. I craved a lot of red meat, which a feller really has to have when he's lost a good deal of blood.

I'd found out the dog's name was Pe-iltzun, or "Buckskin" in English, so I called him Buck. He followed me around as a little puppy might and stayed underfoot much of the time. Not that I minded. After all, he'd saved my life as far as I could see, and I sure enough appreciated that. He and I'd go along with Nell when she hunted, and I learned a lot from them both. Indians never have a lot of cartridges, so they never waste them. I learned how to set snares for the small game like rabbits and gophers. Lizards tasted mighty good the way she prepared them,

and so did snakes. Both of them we killed with willow
switches. Nell said that sometimes it was necessary to eat mice
and pack rats that they'd dig out of their lairs, and they were all
right once you got used to them. After all, they ate mostly
grains and things like that, so the flesh was sweet enough.

One day sticks in my mind. It was about a week after I had
joined up with them. We ran across a steer with one hind leg
busted. He could still get around pretty good and sure was
game, but he was no match for old Buck. That big dog dodged
in past them wicked horns and clamped his teeth in the steer's
upper lip. It didn't take long to wear that critter down to a nub,
even though he swung old Buck around and smacked him into a
tree or two. Before long, the animal was down on his knees, and
then Nell darted in with her knife, slashed his throat with one
swing, and jumped back as he bled out. Buck let go his hold,
growled, and walked stiff-legged around the steer, letting us all
know it had been mostly his doing.

We ate durn good that night, gorging ourselves on all the
meat we could choke down. That was the Indian way, Nell had
told me: Eat all you can when it's available, because you never
know when or where your next meal might come along. I sure
enough tried my best and ate beef until I could hardly budge.
That night, we decided to follow after the two killers. Our for-
tunate find had given us the necessary supplies, so we could
travel fast and not have to stop and hunt food. We made our
plans after supper, deciding to jerk all of the meat we could possibly carry. It was our first opportunity, mayhap the only
opportunity we'd have, and we'd have been fools to let it slip
by without at least trying.

Early the next morning, we began cutting up the steer. I
helped Pop with that, while Nell gathered wood and built up the
racks we needed to hang the meat. It was slow and dirty work,
with flies swarming around us by the thousands. They didn't
seem to bother the old Indian, but they sure got after me.

Nell had sewn me a fine buckskin outfit to wear, and that was
a blessing; otherwise, them flies would've eaten me up in no
time at all. The leggings and shirt were done in a style favored by
the Comanches. Most Apaches had long since taken to wearing

the cotton pants and shirts of the Mexican peons, along with coats or vests, depending upon the weather. Yet with or without pants, they still wore breechclouts. Seems this had some religious meaning, a sort of magic that would protect their private parts. Nell explained that she'd buried all of her husband's clothing, as was their custom, so I would have me a brand-new outfit.

Since she lacked cloth but had plenty of deerskin, she'd decided to make me something similar to what I was accustomed to wearing. Texas punchers wore chaps for protection, so she made me leggings. When I held them up and saw that no seat covering had been included, both Nell and Pop laughed a lot and explained that my rear would be covered by a clout.

She began by going over me with a length of thong, tying knots at various places on the string. She explained to me that the distances between the knots represented my measurements. Once that was done, she began to cut and sew, and in no time at all my outift was ready for me to try on.

Seemed sorta foolish going out behind a tree to put on my new clothes, but I did. After all, Nell must have had ideas about how I looked without clothes, since she'd bathed me a dozen times while I was still sick. Pop came along with me and showed how the breechcloth fitted up under the belt.

The leggings fitted close, running from my waist down to my ankle bone, with the belt sewed on to the tops. They were fringed along the outer seam, long fringes that were mostly for decoration but would help drain off water. The shirt's neckline was V shaped, and it was a pullover. It hung down loosely, about even with my wrists, and the sleeves had long fringes, same as the leggings.

It was a mighty showy outfit, I'll tell you for sure, and I'd never worn anything more comfortable. Both the leggings and the shirt were soft and pliable and didn't bind at all. The moccasins were knee length, like all Apaches wore, but I could fold them down in warm weather. The belt was really a work of art, with intricate stitching and tiny conchos decorating the borders. Nell explained that she had fashioned them from Mexican ten-centavo coins and had scribed on Indian signs. She showed me the tool she'd used. It was like a half of a bullet mold. A punch and a mallet completed the outfit.

The breechcloth was made out of soft doeskin and reached almost to my knees. Nell had stained it a light blue color, using some kind of berry juice, and it looked mighty fine.

I'm afraid I let the old man do most of the work. With a brand-new outfit like mine, it sorta went against the grain to get it all bloodied up in the first week. I taken a deer hide and tied it in front of me sorta like an apron, but I still worked mighty dainty-like. That is, until Pop figured out what was holding me back and grabbed me by the arms. I wound up with his bloody handprints all over both sleeves.

After that, I figured what the heck and dived right into the carcass, cutting away for all I was worth. We cut that critter up in long strips no more'n a quarter of an inch in thickness. That way, the flies might cluster on it, but the meat was too thin for them to lay their eggs. In two days, according to Nell, the meat would dry to a rock-hard consistency and would keep for a long time. I'd gnawed on a lot of jerky in my time and knew it could keep a man going for a long ways. If we had time to cook, then soaking it in water would cause it to swell, and with the addition of some wild onions or whatever was available, we'd have us a tasty stew. The whole job taken us less than three hours.

We'd held out the loins along with a few choice steaks that would be eaten that day. Nell had wrapped green leaves around the steer's tongue and buried it under the coals of the previous night's fire. The liver she hung over the heat on some green sticks. While we were working on the meat, we all had tender chunks of tongue and steaming hot liver. Just shows you how quickly a man can change his habits. Until then, my tastes in eating had been considerably different. Man who's really hungry will eat most anything and pay no mind to how it's been prepared. Laying around bunkhouses and taking my meals off the tailboard of a chuck wagon, I'd heard tales how fellers lost in the wilderness chewed bark off of trees and turned over rocks, eating whatever they found under them. I reckon it's mostly what you're used to. Why, I can remember back when I was a youngster, I never could eat turnips, parsnips, or rutabagas, all of which my maw grew in her garden. Believe me, there came a time when all of them roots tasted like candy to me. So you see, that's like this liver that Nell barely cooked. Hell, the blood was still dripping from it. But it was delicious! Like my maw, most roundup cooks would fry liver until it curled up at the edges. I'd never been able to stomach any of that, but I had considered half-soling my boots with a couple of slices; they were that hard and toughened by overcooking. Honest to betcha!

After we'd gotten all the meat strips hung upon the racks Nell had made, it was time to clean up. Buck had walked off into the brush with a big bone I'd given him, and we tossed the rest out where other animals could get at it. My shoulder was aching, and I itched all over. I called out to Nell and told her I was going down to the creek to bathe.

"Take the rifle," she said. "You might see a deer or an antelope or even a turkey. We can always use more meat."

She was busy repacking some of the hide pouches and had plenty to do. I picked up the Winchester carbine and looked to be sure it had a round in the chamber. Waving back at her, I set out for the creek some three hundred yards away. There was a good reason for not camping on the creek's bank; matter of fact, two good reasons. Flash floods were common in those canyons, and while you might get out with no more'n a good drenching, you'd usually lose your outfit. Second, an enemy searching for water could accidentally stumble onto your camp and kill you in your sleep. That had almost happened to me, I thought to myself ruefully.

I felt a lot stronger and had regained almost all the strength in my left arm. The work we'd done had helped me a great deal, not only physically but also mentally. Made me feel like I was at least earning my keep, and to me that was important. Some fellers rode the grubline, so to speak. It didn't bother them to follow a regular route, stopping by at ranches and taking advantage of the hospitality that was a sorta unwritten law in the Western lands. They'd make halfhearted attempts to get a job, but they weren't really looking for work, just for a handout. Me, I never could do a thing like that. If I ate at a man's table, then I made darn sure I chopped some wood or mended some fence or did something so's it wasn't charity. In this case, of course, there sure hadn't been much I could do, being all busted up and not in shape to do much of anything. But now. . . . Heck, I mused. I had been about to say to myself that I'd pay these folks back in full. I'm going to marry that girl, I thought. She may not believe it to be true, leastways not right now. She might have thought I was still fevered when I said what I did. Figured I was locoed then. Like I'd told her, she was the most beautiful girl I had ever laid eyes on, and I was going to make her mine. We could get us a little piece of land and start from scratch.

There you go, I told myself. Talking big again, and not a darn thing to back it up! Right now you'd best figure in terms of getting back that wagon, along with the rest of your possessions. You ain't able to take care of yourself right now, much less taking on a wife, and her not too long from having a child.

That was another thing. Was I ready to take on a family? Because that's what it would amount to. A ready-made family! Not only a red Injun baby but the old feller, too. Can't just pull out and leave him behind, I told myself. How're you going to handle that, Jake Bailey? Appears to me you're about to get in deeper than you can afford.

Out of the corner of my eye I'd gotten a glimpse of some dun-colored critter off to one side in the brush. Looked a mite bigger'n a coyote and too low to the ground for a deer or antelope. The cover was so dense, I could only see a bit of color and movement, no more. Whatever it was, the animal was headed toward the creek.

A small knoll was off to one side. From on top, I'd have a better view and might be able to get in a decent shot. I trotted toward it, holding the carbine in front of me to ward off the branches. It was mighty hot in the thicket, and that little bit of running had me breathing hard, like a dogie calf hunting for its mama.

I reckon all that thrashing and my heavy breathing turned that critter around, and he was headed right for me when I topped that knoll. It was one of them Mexican pumas, with his jaw hanging down, and showing a mouthful of teeth. Ears laid back, he was about three steps from making his leap as I raised the carbine and squeezed the trigger.

Well sir, he let out a yowl, you could've heard in East Texas! That first shot hit him right square in the brisket, and he spun around and started running. I worked the lever down and chambered another round. My second shot struck in behind a shoulder and tumbled him end over end, but he sure didn't let it bother him none. Up he sprang, and once more he came right at me, lips pulled back from bared teeth and spittle drooling down both sides of his mouth. His tail was lashing back and forth stiffly, and from his throat I heard a guttural, drawn-out moan, an angry, hurt sound that shook me to the core. Dead on his feet, he meant to take me along with him. Eyes burning with hate, he kept on coming.

I stood my ground, working the lever and firing from the hip. Twice he stumbled but recovered; then the fifth shot nailed him in an eye, and he crashed to the ground, twitched a time or two, then lay still. He wasn't no more'n fifteen feet in front of me, and he was plenty big. I guessed maybe he'd have weighed out at somewheres around two hundred, and that's a mighty big cat, let me tell you for sure!

I was still standing there breathing hard, with my heart going a mile a minute, when Nell showed up with Pop trailing her by fifty feet. Remembering, I carefully let the hammer down to the safety cock and knelt to take a closer look.

My hands are overly large for my size, but the pads that cat walked on were half again as big. His claws were longer than my middle finger and sharp as razors. If I hadn't had the luck to stop him, he'd have laid me open from throat to crotch! Gave me the shivers just thinking about it. He was a young lion in spite of his great size, because he had all of his teeth, and they were white as ivory. I stood up and looked at him in awe. I'd seen a few cougars in working the Texas brush, but never one this huge. Leaning over, I tried to span his length with my arms outstretched. Like I said earlier, my arms are overlong, and my reach is some six feet. Hard as I tried, I couldn't span his length from the nose to the root of his tail. That alone was at least four feet long. Overall, he was more'n eleven feet long. More'n likely, he'd killed and eaten many a deer in his time.

"Are you all right?" Nell asked anxiously. "Did you get hurt, Jake?" She was looking me over, her concern making me self-conscious. I handed her the carbine and asked for the loan of her knife.

"We'd best git him skinned out," I told her. "No tellin' who might come runnin' after hearin' all them shots. You 'n' Pop can give me a hand if you like, but I want to keep this hide for myself." I raised one of the paws. "Mebbe you'd like to hang on to these here claws. They'd sure enough make a mighty pretty necklace."

Suddenly, for no apparent reason, she grabbed hold of me and hugged me for all she was worth. I bent down and kissed her lips. For a moment she responded; then she tore her arms loose and stepped back, breathing hard.

CHAPTER 7

THAT NIGHT, I HAD TROUBLE GOING TO SLEEP. I LAY there a couple of hours thinking of all that had happened that day and remembering how soft Nell's lips had felt. That is, until she had begun to respond.

Supper had been awkward, with little conversation between us. The old man had made up for it by chattering away for all he was worth. It was like he was trying to make up for some of those years when he'd been without friends. At first I couldn't make out much of what he was saying, but after some time I got to where I could understand, and we yarned away, in a sort of Injun-English. A lot of hand waving went on, a real necessity when you needed to emphasize a point.

He told me about some of the lone trails he'd taken and how he'd always been able to make off with a few horses. He never did get around to mentioning that last raid, but I had an idea he wanted to talk about it, wanted to tell someone.

"We'd sat there a little ways back from the fire, smoking our pipes, each one trying to outdo the other with some tall tale. I had a few of them myself, and one or two made the old man

laugh. It was like we'd known each other all our lives, a warm
feeling, let me tell you! A stranger who might have happened
along probably would have thought it strange, this closeness we
were sharing. There I was, an overgrown East Texas younker,
laughing and carrying on with this wizened, little old man like
we were old saddle pards.

Hell, he was old enough to be my grandpaw! But that was not
important somehow. I remembered my own grandpaw pretty
well. I was only about seven when he passed on. A mustang
bronc had tried his best to stomp a mudhole in him, and he'd
never gotten well. Lingered on for almost a year before cashing
in his chips. It's funny, but I wasn't never able to be close to
him, not like I was with the old Indian. 'Course, I was pretty
young then, and I reckon that made a difference.

My paw had passed on about a year later. He found him an
unbranded calf, roped it, and got down off his horse to put on
his brand. He'd never even gotten his fire lighted. One of the
hands found him lying there, a little pile of sticks and brush
nearby and a cinch ring in his hand. That calf's old mama had
gotten a horn into him, and he'd bled to death. Horse had
spooked and run off, dragging the calf behind him. The old cow
had followed, trying to get her dead calf to stand. I'd cried
when they brought Paw home and again that next morning
when they laid him to rest alongside of my grandpaw.

Maw taken the easiest course she could think of by getting
herself married up with our foreman. It was either that or sell
the place, I guess. She couldn't run it by herself. I had never
much cared for that feller, and I reckon it showed pretty plain.
He was hell on horses and men alike but got the job done, and
that's all my paw had wanted from him. He was a big brute of a
man and thought nothing of beating the men when he chose to.
One had tried to face him down with a six-gun but died before
his gun cleared the holster. Six of the hands asked for their time
the day he married Maw, and the rest drifted off one by one.

Being a younker, there wasn't much else I could do. With
Maw blind to some of his bullying tactics and ignoring most of
the rest, I just had to hang in there and wait for something to
turn up, for someone to put him in his place.

By the time I was ten, I was doing a man's work and getting no pay for it. It was enough that he fed me and put a roof over my head, or so he told me. Once he taken me into the barn and whupped me with a lead rope. I can't remember what it was that I'd done to deserve it—some little thing. I never cried, not one single tear, and when he was done, I told him I'd kill him if he ever touched me again. I guess he believed me, because I never got another beating. He had other ways to put me in my place. I got all the dirty jobs the other men wouldn't touch unless there was no way to get out of them. Pulling out bogged cattle became my specialty, and I doubt my boots were ever dry. Whenever we had to move cattle, I always rode the drag, and at roundup time I pulled double shifts at night guard.

I had me a fine horse in my string, what was called a *bayo coyote*, a true buckskin with the black mustang stripe down his backbone, along with a black mane, hooves, and tail. I'd taken more care with him and used to sneak him little grain handouts every now and then. He'd turned out to be a great cutting horse and even better as a roper. I roped many a coyote from his back, and he never let one get in close.

He wasn't a real big horse, probably didn't weigh no more than nine hundred pounds, but he was all heart! I cared for that horse more'n I cared for anything or anybody, and the day my stepfather said he was taking him for his own, I went plumb loco. Before he knowed what was in my mind, I'd shook out a loop and dabbed it over his shoulders.

The buckskin backed right down and jerked him off his feet. Every time he tried to get up, the horse taken up the slack, and down he'd go again. At first he cussed me and called me everything but a white man. Then he began pleading, promising to treat me square if I turned him loose. I let on like I couldn't hear a word he was saying, leaning my hands on the saddle horn and grinning down at him.

Maw came out on the porch and hollered at me, asking for me to let him go, saying that if I wasn't careful, I might kill him for sure. I knew what he'd do if I did let him up, and I had no hankering to die so young, So I just wheeled that horse around and taken out for the far yonder, with him bouncing and bumping along behind me, screaming and hollering for the Good Lord to help him, for anybody to please save him!

We drug him out about a quarter mile and then stopped. I had no intention of killing him and having to run from the law for the rest of my life. He was out cold, all scratched and tore up like he'd taken on a bobcat, but he wasn't dead. I stepped down and loosed my rope, coiling it up and putting it back where it belonged. For a moment I stood there and looked down at him. I'd never see him again, nor would the ranch ever be mine. I felt bad about leaving Maw, but I had to; there was no other choice. I was twelve years old.

That had been ten years ago, and I'd seen a lot of Texas since then. Other places, too: Abilene, the Indian Nations, and Fort Smith, over in Arkansas. I'd been to Denver, where just last year it had become the new territorial capital, a busy city with more'n four thousand folks living there.

Now, here I was in New Mexico Territory with a brand-new friend and a girl I loved dearly. I'd told them that story about leaving the home ranch, and they'd listened with great sympathy, knowing from their own experience how hard it is to leave your home behind.

"What brought you to New Mexico?" Nell asked. "There are not many cattle here, only the white men who mine gold and copper from the mountains. You're not a miner, and that is the only work for white men around here. This is not an easy land. Water is not plentiful, and grasslands not easily found. Cattle would do well, I believe, if a man had the experience and knowledge of the land, but few have tried."

I'd already explained that my wagon held mining equipment I was delivering to a mine near Lordsburg. What I planned after that I really didn't know, and I told them that.

"Reason I went to Denver City," I said, "was because the boss taken a herd up there to sell to the miners. I worked the herd like the rest of the fellers, but I had me an idea. I'd planned to haul freight in Colorado, but that deal turned out to be a bad one. So I came on down to Santa Fe and wound up with the haul to Lordsburg. Heck, Nell! Just like I told you before, I've been sort of a wanderin' man all of my life. Always lookin' to see what's on the other side of the mountains. Now, things could be different with someone like you to take care of. I'd be different; you'd see.''

That had sort of ended our conversation, and she had gone to her shelter on the far side of the clearing. She hadn't been feeling all that well and wanted to get some sleep. I needed sleep, too, but wasn't having much luck doing so. In the morning, we would take the trail of the killers, and the more rest I could get, the better. I yawned.

Soft footsteps in the sandy soil brought me bolt upright. I stared. It was Nell, wrapped in a blanket and standing beside my pallet. She bent down and kissed me softly for a long moment; then, standing upright, she spoke.

"We must wait," she told me. "Wait until we have caught up with the two white men and avenged my husband's death.''

She turned and was gone, silently, like a ghost in the darkness. I stared up at the stars and tasted her sweetness on my lips. I *will* wait, I breathed quietly. I would wait for her to choose the time, but I hoped it would not be too much longer. I sighed and turned over on my side. In a moment I was sound asleep, dreaming of huge, green pastures and my Nell on a pure white horse. She was smiling at me, and that made everything all right again!

We were on our way before daylight, heading back to where I'd had my last camp, where them two skunks had tried their durndest to kill me. From there, we figured it'd be easy to pick up the wagon tracks. I was hoping they would stick together for a time, because wagon ruts would be a lot easier to follow than horse and mule tracks. Besides, horse tracks would mean we'd have to make a choice about which set to follow. It was a cinch we couldn't split up. We had only that one gun, and I wasn't about to let Nell or Pop off by themselves.

Me 'n' Buck led the way, though in truth I was following a trail of which I had no recollection. The dog trotted along easily and seemed to know where he was going. I was carrying the .44 Winchester with the magazine fully loaded, plus a buckskin bag of extra cartridges that hung over the horn. We weren't exactly ready for an all-out war, but I never expected to play fair. We'd take whatever advantage we could, and that didn't include giving neither one of them devils an even break. I'd shoot them down on sight, like any animal.

The big sorrel I was riding was a powerful horse with an easy stride. It had belonged to Nell's husband and had been his pride and joy, according to her. He'd stolen the animal on a raid into Mexico, along with the fancy *charro* saddle I was straddling. Strips of the original owner's hair were decorating the cheek-straps of the headstall and had been woven in the bit. The red stud didn't give me any sass when I caught him up, and that surprised me at first. Then I realized that my clothing was made from Indian-cured buckskin and had him fooled.

Nell was close behind on a little chestnut mare, and old Pop brought up our rear. He had himself about the sorriest, ugliest old gelding I ever had seen! Rib-sprung and cow-hocked, with a long ewe neck, it looked to be on the verge of collapse. Trailing behind on a long rawhide lead were two burros loaded down with all our gear. I guess by that time I considered myself part of the band, 'cause I considered it "our" gear, but in truth that was how I felt.

Like most young boys on the frontier, I had wished that I could be an Indian. Not always, of course. Not when they'd just raided a nearby ranch and killed everybody. Then I'd wanted to be a Texas Ranger so's I could spend time chasing after the Indians. I reckon the wild life has always had an appeal for boys of all ages and in most places. Before Paw was killed, me 'n' another boy from a neighboring ranch used to play Injun. We'd ride our ponies down by the river, hide our saddles and clothes in the brush, and ride around in our underdrawers, whooping and hollering and pretending we were raiding Comanches. Those were sure good times!

The dog was prancing around, tongue lolling, a low growling sound coming from his throat. I peered ahead and could see a clearing that looked familiar. We were there! Here I had made my last camp, nearly the last one, as it turned out.

A warning sound from Pop made me turn. He had pushed up and handed the burros' lead to Nell. He motioned me to stay where I was and wait for him to scout the clearing. For an old man he was surprisingly agile. Sliding down off his mount, he went ahead of us, leading the horse. We waited in there for perhaps half an hour before he returned.

In one hand he carried a pair of ragged pants. Made out of faded blue wool, with a yellow stripe down the legs, they were soldier's pants, cavalry by the stripe. Pop handed me the pants. "So'jer," he said. "Pony so'jer." He pointed to one of the pockets, and I thrust my hand inside. I found a dirty piece of paper, wrinkled and stained with sweat.

Squinting against the overhead sun, I peered at the writing I'd found. It was a death sentence! One Stephen Braunt had been found guilty of murdering a Sergeant Charles Wilkerson and had been sentenced to be shot by firing squad. The date was August 12, 1869, and the sentence was to be carried out at a time and place to be decided at a later date.

In the same pocket I found a bronze button with crossed sabers and the word "Sixth." The heading on the paper read HEADQUARTERS—FORT MCRAE, DEPARTMENT OF NEW MEXICO. I gave the paper to Nell. "One of them, probably both, was under a death sentence," I said. "No wonder they were so ornery."

I turned to Pop and asked what else he had found. After all, we weren't all that interested in what they'd done to a sergeant, whatever his name. We wanted them for what they'd done to us. If they were of a mind, the Army could put what was left of them in the ground after we'd done our part.

The old man was talking fairly fast, so Nell interpreted to speed things up. "The Old One says they left this clearing together. One man is riding a horse, and the other sits in the wagon, with a mule following behind. He tracked them for a quarter mile, and they appear to be heading southwest. Where he left their track, there are two canyons: one that's easily followed to the west, and the other, a more difficult route, takes you to the southwest and eventually Mexico!

"If they intended to go west, they'd have taken the more easily traveled trail. So that means they are heading for a small town on the Gila, where they will try to get rid of the machinery in the wagon. They'll need money if they've got Mexico in mind as a sanctuary. No gringo can live for nothing, and jobs are not plentiful for non-Mexicans.''

Here old Pop interrupted her and pointed a finger while a torrent of words spilled from his mouth. Nell nodded in agreement, it seemed, and turned back to me. "If they don't abandon the wagon,'' she said, "we have a good chance to make up some of the time we've lost. It means taking some risks, but it could be worth it. Let me explain.'' She knelt down and smoothed out a patch of sandy ground.

"We are about here,'' she told me, drawing a small circle. About eighteen inches away she drew a wavy line and another circle about midway on that line. "The line is the Gila River,'' she said, "and the circle is a small village called Red Rock. It isn't far from here, maybe sixty miles if you can fly like a bird. The mountains have many cross-canyons, and it is impossible for a wagon to go in a straight line.''

"They must follow the canyons,'' she went on, "and then travel like this.'' She drew another wavy line, one that went down and up, down and up, down and up, repeating this until the drawing looked more like a child's scribble than a map.

"Eventually, they will come out on the flats within four miles of Red Rock, but it could take them many days, maybe a week or more if they move only during the daylight hours.''

I stared at her incredulously. "What does five or six days mean, even a week? They taken my wagon about two weeks back. They're in Arizona by now, mebbe halfway to Tucson! We'll git 'em all right, but it's gonna take time! A lotta time. There jest ain't no shortcuts, Nell.''

She shook her head. "No. I don't agree.'' With one of her fingers, she drew circles in several places, all of them southwest of our position. "These are the locations of some Army forts,'' she told me, a big grin on her face. "All have soldiers patrolling constantly. Those men will have to stay clear of them or take a chance of being recaptured. We're not tied down like that, not with you with us. No soldiers will bother us or try to take us back to the reservation as runaways if you explain what we are doing.

"Tell me," she went on. "How much food did you carry? A lot? Say, enough to last you for a week or more?"

"Sure," I replied. "I figgered mebbe some of them miners might be hard up for grub. I bought me five cases of tinned peaches and tomatoes, all in airtights, that I figgered they would buy at a good price. Along with them, I carried a few slabs of bacon, two sacks of beans, and some flour. Why?"

She grinned again and explained patiently. "Those men think you are dead. From the beating you described, plus a bullet at close range, most men *would* be dead. They must be feeling very safe about now. They know that I can't report them to the Army, so they've no worries on that score. Food isn't an immediate problem, because they are well supplied."

She stood up, arms akimbo, and looked me in the eye. "I say we go like the birds. There!" She pointed off, toward a distant peak. "We can't fly, but we can go straight," she said. "With the horses, we can cross these mountains in two days. Once across, we'll look for the wagon tracks. If the tracks can't be found, then we'll know those killers are not out of the canyons, and we can wait for them. Set up an ambush and shoot them down like they deserve. Now! What do you say to that, Jake Bailey?"

What the heck could I say? She had it all planned out, a plan that didn't seem to have any hitches as far as I could see. "We'll do it," I cried. "Durn tootin', we will! Jest one little favor first, and then I'll go along with everything you've said. You 'n' Pop git started on over thet mountain, and I'll be along directly. I'm gonna make sure they stayed together as best I can. I'll foller their sign for a few miles. Might even find where they made the first camp stop. It could be they wanted to git away a few miles and then split up. I'll catch up with you'n Pop before night."

Nell wasn't sure it was a good idea, but I talked her into it. I explained that my horse was stronger, and I'd have no trouble overtaking them. "Besides," I told her, "there is a chance that you might be wrong, thet they wanted some miles in back of them before they divided up my gear. This way, we'll know for sure. You go on now, and I'll be right in behind you." I wanted

badly to kiss her, but it wasn't a thing you did in plain sight of
God and everybody. Not that old Pop would've minded. I was
sure of that!

I waited until they had a good start, then turned my redskin
sorrel stud down the canyon to my left. The wagon sign was
plain to see—deep ruts, with sand sifted into them—and the
tracks of my stolen saddle horse and pack mule showed up almost as plainly. The rider was off to one side, while the mule
was tied on behind.

About an hour down the trail, I found where they had left the
wagon and built a fire nearby. They had unhitched and put the
four animals out to graze. A whole bacon rind showed how
hungry they must have been. It was covered with big black
ants, as were some bread crusts lying nearby. I also saw where
they had bedded down from the blanket marks in the sand. I
cussed when I found the empty whiskey bottle. Them sons!
They'd drunk my good whiskey. The whole damn bottle!

Well, so far Nell had been right about everything. It did look
like they figured on keeping the wagon, and that should fit right
into her plans. What the heck!

I wheeled the red stud around and raced back up the canyon.
He sure enough wanted to run and wasn't all that happy when I
turned him up the slope in the direction she had picked out.
Their tracks were plain to see—scuff marks and turned dirt
where their horses had tried for a footing.

CHAPTER 8

WE SPENT THE FIRST NIGHT IN A LITTLE HOLLOW
that was hidden in back of an outcropping of rock. Maybe millions of years back that portion of the earth had groaned and burst skyward, leaving this thin, flat shelf of rock that resembled a shed roof. It was a perfect spot, and we lost no time taking advantage of it.

Pop got out his fire-making materials, and Nell started to shave some of our jerked beef into a pot, while me 'n' the dog made sure we were all by our loneselves. Buck sniffed out a half dozen marmot dens, growled when he found one occupied, but finally gave his stamp of approval to our campsite.

I'd caught up with them in midafternoon and related all I had found, including the empty whiskey bottle. "They must feel safe enough," I told Nell. "Just as you said, it looks like they figger I'm dead and they got nothin' to fear. In fact, from the way the sign read, they ain't in no hurry at all! Them animals were at a walk. Bein' half starved, they may jest take their own sweet time and try gittin' some of the wrinkles out of their bellies. On my grub," I added.

The old man had built a smokeless fire, one you could cup in
your hand, if it was that small, but it seemed to do the job just
fine. In no time at all, Nell had us a big beef stew with greens
and herbs she'd picked up along the way. After it had cooked,
she set it off to one side to keep warm so she could put the coffeepot on to boil.

I sat up on top while all this was being done so no one could
sneak up and catch us unawares. Pop had told me this wasn't
necessary. He'd already scouted out the area and saw no reason
for a guard being kept. Still, I felt it was better to be safe than
sorry. I'd already been caught unaware by them two killers and
didn't want it repeated. Besides, being alone up there gave me a
chance to study things out.

Though Nell had been half joking when she remarked on me
not having anything to trade for a bride, still, she had hit the
nail on the head. Unless I could get back my wagon and my animals, I was flat busted. There wasn't any way I could make a
start with a family, not on a cowpuncher's pay. With Nell expecting a baby, we would have to at least have a roof over our
heads. All them dreams of locating on our own land would be
just that—dreams!

With the money I stood to gain by delivering that mining machinery, we'd be able to build us a cabin and have enough to get
by until I could put a small herd together. If hard work was all it
it would take, it'd be a different story. Land was there for the
taking, and cattle were running wild all over the place. Horses,
too! I could maybe run down a few, rough-break them, and sell
them to the Army. There were all sorts of ways to earn a living,
but it took time. We had to have that stake first, or we'd just flat
never make it.

I'd seen many a feller try to get by. With women scarce in the
territories, more'n one cowpoke had married up with a saloon
girl. One of them "soiled doves," as the churchgoing folks
called them. Lots of those marriages worked out just fine.

Hell! If marrying Nell meant I might have to milk a cow or
even raise chickens, I'd do it, by golly! If scratching like a
chicken was the only way I could win her, I'd run on down to

the blacksmith and have me a pair of spurs made up so's I could get out there and scratch with the best of 'em.

Whoa up, cowboy! Ain't you taking a lot for granted? I asked myself. A kiss don't mean all that much, and besides that, it was more like a sisterly kiss, anyways. Or was it? She did say we had ought to wait for a spell and for me to be patient with her. To give her more time! It was her did the hugging, not me, and it had surprised the heck outta me!

About that time, Nell called up and said that supper was ready to eat, so I quit my daydreaming and slid on down to where they were waiting. I was as hungry as a lobo wolf.

While we were eating, the old man mentioned that we could expect a nearly full moon that night and suggested that we ride on as soon as it was light enough to see the trail. I agreed, and so did Nell, and after supper we settled down to wait.

I helped clean up the dishes and pack away the supplies; then Nell and I climbed up to where I'd been sitting earlier, on top of the rocky shelf. I had a whole lot to say to her but really didn't know where to begin. Pop came on up just a few minutes later, carrying something in his hand.

It looked to be a length of hollowed-out log about four or five inches in diameter and eighteen inches long. There were two strings spanning the slightly curved log, and as we watched, Pop plucked at them and made a sound somewhat the same as a banjo. I started to say something, but Nell put a hand on my arm and squeezed slightly. I turned and saw a finger at her lips, cautioning me to be silent.

The old man hunkered down and put one end of the log between his feet, holding the other end with one hand. He had what looked like a short, curved bow in the other hand, with a taut string. Bending his head, he began sawing away, producing an eerie, plaintive melody the likes of which I had never heard before.

At first, it was irritating, but then I found myself swaying in time to the music and liking what I heard. Automatically, I began patting my hands on my thighs, and a moment later so did Nell. I forgot where we were and what we had to do, letting go of all my tensions and losing myself in the magic of the music

he played. My eyes were closed, and I felt drowsy. Suddenly
the tempo changed, and the beat picked up! My hands hit my
thighs faster, and I felt warmer, while at the same time chills
were running up and down my spine. Faster and faster he
played, until I found it hard to breath, and the blood pumping
through my neck veins threatened to choke me!

Then he stopped playing, and the silence was so complete
that I could hear my own heartbeat. Beside me, Nell's breath
was coming in gasps, and she clutched at my arm as I tried hard
to catch my breath.

"What was thet?" I gasped. "Ain't never heard no fiddler
play like thet! Why, it made me want to git up and dance.
Dance like I never danced before. How'd he do thet, Nell?"

She turned to me, her eyes shining, glistening with moisture
from unshed tears. "He honors you, Jake Bailey. That music
has never been heard by any white man. When a warrior band is
planning a raid, it is used to stir their anger and to make them
ready for battle. But the first part, the even and soulful music,
that was an appeal to his gods."

"Well sir," I said. "I don't recollect ever hearin' music like
thet before, nor nothin' even close to it. It sure as heck had me
goin' strong. It was beautiful but sorta scary, too. I had goose
bumps bigger'n hen's eggs on my back! What can I say to him,
Nell? Hadn't I ought to thank him or at least tell him how much
I liked it?"

She shook her head. "No, Jake. He knows without saying
anything." She smiled. "You were really carried away by the
sounds, Jake! You should have seen yourself. Like a man pos-
sessed by spirits; you were swaying and patting your legs so
fast that your hands were a blur. I'm glad that it pleased you,
Jake. It makes us closer somehow."

I grinned and squeezed her hand. "You should've looked in
a mirror, Nell. You were doin' the same as me, mebbe even
faster! I don't reckon nobody could sit still if they heard music
like thet." I leaned forward and kissed her on the mouth gently,
then released her hand and stood up.

"We'd best be on our way," I told her. "We'll ride until
midnight, then find us a place to roll up for a few hours."

A three-quarter moon was lighting the ridges and showing the trail well enough for us to ride on. In minutes we had the horses saddled and were on our way. With any luck, the mountains could be crossed in two days, and we'd know how we stood as far as catching up with the killers. Even if they had made it out of the canyons, we'd still be gaining a week of travel on them and be that much closer to sweet revenge.

I was carrying the rifle across my saddle bow, and with a start, I realized I was squeezing the stock so tightly that it hurt my hand. Damn them skunks! Them dirty, motherless, no good sons! If I'd had them there, that very moment, we'd have had no more to worry about, 'cause they'd be dead! I'd kill them with my bare hands if need be and think no more about it than if I'd stepped on a bug!

CHAPTER 9

ABOUT NOON THE SECOND DAY WE SAW A COLUMN of smoke rising out of a canyon to the west. It looked to be some two miles away as the crow flies, and it forced us to make our first change of plans.

"It can't be them," I said, "but still, we dassn't take a chance. No sense in all of us ridin' on over there. Let me jest take a little look-see and make sure. Could be it's a patrol of soldiers fixin' their noon coffee. Won't hurt to talk to them and find out if they've seen the wagon tracks. You two go on, and I'll ketch up with you soon's I find out what's over there. Agreed?"

Nell had some objections, but Pop saw the sense in what I was saying. "You go, Jeke," he told me. "We see you there, by *tinaja*." He pointed ahead a mile or so, where a pond of water could be seen and some scrub trees. He dug a heel in his scrawny horse and rode off, Nell following behind with the burros in tow. Looking back over her shoulder, she waved. I raised my hand, then turned toward the smoke.

It was rough going and mostly downhill, with loose shale making the footing treacherous. When I got within a quarter mile or so, I decided to leave my horse behind and come up to the fire on foot. With my Apache boots, I could be fairly certain of not making a lot of noise in the gravel.

I slipped out the horse's bit and let it dangle under his chin so that he could graze more comfortably; I gave him a twenty-foot length or so of picket rope.

With the rifle held at the ready, I started walking. The smoke could be seen plainly, rising straight up just around a bend in the canyon. Striding in close to the canyon wall, I made my way toward that bend. Reaching it, I peered past a rocky spire and saw my saddle horse tied up to a tree. My pack mule was just beyond, stripping leaves from a scrub oak tree with his teeth and munching them noisily.

I'd never seen the man hunkered down by the fire, but the hat he was wearing was mine, and so was the jacket. No wagon was in sight, but I had to make sure the man was alone.

Carefully, I backed up and scanned the canyon wall for a way up. If I could get above him, I'd be able to see everything a lot better and make sure the other man, the one who had the beard, wasn't close by with the wagon. There wasn't any way up that I could see, so I decided to take the risk.

Catfooting back to the bend, I taken another look. There wasn't any way I could get in closer without being seen. A thin trickle of water ran in a sandy wash about midway down the center of the canyon, but the wash wasn't deep enough to conceal me, even if I could get to it, without being spotted by the man at the fire.

Offhand, I estimated the range to be about sixty yards, a chancy shot with the short carbine unless I could drop him with the first round. He would have plenty of cover in the event I only wounded him, and we could easily wind up with a Mexican standoff, him bedded down in the trees and me forced to stay behind the rocks. There was still at least seven hours of daylight left, and I could get mighty thirsty with my canteen back where I'd left the horse.

A coffeepot sat on a flat rock next to the fire, and as I watched, he reached out for the handle and poured himself a cup, then sat back sipping from the rim. Damn him! That was my pot, my cup, and my coffee!

Easing back the carbine's hammer, I slipped the barrel in a notch between the spire and the canyon's wall. With the front sight centered in the rear, I aimed at a point just in front of his right ear. With him quartering toward me, the bullet should strike somewhere in the head or chest, depending on how much the slug would drop or how much the sights varied.

When it came time to squeeze the trigger, I couldn't! In spite of my hatred, in spite of all the man had done to me and to Nell, I couldn't kill him in cold blood. I tried to pull that trigger, believe me, but I just couldn't do it.

Drawing back the carbine, I let the hammer down and lowered the butt to the ground. I'd have to give him a warning of some kind, give him a chance to surrender. But suppose he did surrender. What could I do then? Taking him over to where Nell and the old man were waiting would have been like bringing in a rabid skunk. Pop would haved killed him in a minute without batting an eye. No! I'd give him a warning, but only a chance to defend himself. I'd call him out and let it be a fair fight. My conscience couldn't argue with that.

Cocking the carbine, I aimed carefully and shot the pot off the rock, just to get his attention. Then I hollered at him and told him to stand up and keep his hands out where I could see them. "You reach for a gun," I told him, "and I promise you'll be a dead man. Now, move! Damn you, move!"

For a moment he just sat there, hunkered over that fire, staring. Not at me but at the coffeepot. My shot had knocked it into the fire, and steam was rising from the spilled coffee and circling up around his head. As I stepped out from behind the rocks, he looked up without seeming to recognize me, but he stayed on his haunches.

"Who in hell are you anyways?" he cried out. "What call you got shootin' up a man's coffeepot? You crazy or what? I ain't never laid eyes on you, mister, and I sure ain't got no mind to be kilt over nuthin'!"

"I'm the man you robbed two weeks back. Do you remember thet, you skunk? I could've shot you jest as easy as I did the coffeepot, but I ain't no murderer, not like you 'n' thet partner of yours! You beat a man to death and left behind a widow, and her carryin' his baby! If she hadn't picked up thet rifle and run you off, you'd've killed her, too.

"Then you found me asleep in my blankets and tried your best to beat me to death. Figgered you had, or you wouldn't be sittin' here now. You'd be hightailin' it for the nearest hidey-hole like the cowardly coyote you are. Now, I'm gonna tell you once more. Git on your feet or I'll shoot a hole in you big enough to ride a horse through!"

He was scared, no doubt of that. He got to his feet, his eyes darting to both sides, looking for a way out. Hands in the air, he pleaded with me.

"It weren't me, mister. I didn't touch you, I swear! It was the other man, not me. He's the one who used the chain. I tried to talk him out of it. Told him we'd jist take your stuff and to leave you be. He wouldn't listen to me!"

As I walked slowly toward him, his eyes kept glancing at the ground. Right next to where he'd been sitting, the butt of a rifle was showing. I stopped twenty yards away, and I pointed the muzzle of the carbine toward the gun.

"Go ahead," I told him. "Pick it up. Carefully, though, or I'll blow a hole in your guts. I'm gonna give you a fair shake, but we're gonna do it my way. You jest pick it up by the barrel and hold it out at arm's length. Careful, now!"

"I don't want to fight you, mister. I ain't no damn fool of a kid. I know what you're plannin' to do. Soon's I have that gun in my hands, you're gonna shoot me and say it happened in self-defense. G'wan! If you're gonna kill me for somethin' I didn't do, then you go on and do it. Shoot me!"

For a moment I was distracted, and he dived to the ground, rolling over with the rifle in his hands. It boomed, and I felt a hot pain lance across my shoulder as I dropped to my knees, triggering the carbine from my hip. Through the powder smoke, I saw him grab at his middle with both hands and drop the rifle down on the ground. He bent over nearly double, clutching at his belly, then slowly fell backward and lay there groaning, legs twitching and heels dug into the dirt. Blood flowed between his fingers as he stared up at me with terror-stricken eyes.

"You've kilt me! God damn yuh, you've kilt me! Go on, do it again. Shoot me in the head. I'm dyin' anyways, and it hurts." He closed his eyes and rolled his head over to one side, his face contorted with pain. I jacked the empty case out of the carbine, levering a fresh round into the chamber, and lowered the hammer to half cock. "Not jest yet, feller," I told him. "You 'n' me, we got us some talkin' to do."

The wound in my shoulder was just a graze. I pulled down the neck of my hunting shirt and found a bloody groove the width of my finger. It stung a mite, but it'd already stopped bleeding. I'd have Nell put some of her salve on it.

The wounded man was right; he was dying. It might take a while, but he was beyond any help from me. The heavy bullet had flattened and had torn away part of his spine, leaving an exit wound the size of my fist. There was no way I could stop it from bleeding. Squatting down there, I looked him over. He was the one who'd beaten Nell's husband to death, I reckoned. Leastways, he wasn't the man with the gold tooth and a heavy black beard, the one who'd used the chain on me.

He looked to be about my height and weight but not quite as wide in the shoulders or long in the arms. His hair was sorta dirty blond and shaggy, curling over his ears and on his collar. He'd shaved recently, like maybe two days ago, and a light stubble covered his cheeks and chin. That made me wonder where my razor might be. Maybe in his pockets, along with some of my other stuff.

To tell the truth, I sorta hated to touch him, much less go through his pockets. The clothes were mine, but I didn't want them back—not now. Somehow the thought of his filthy body even touching them turned my stomach. I'd bury him in the whole outfit, boots and all! I shook his shoulder.

"Where's your partner, and where's my wagon? Tell me or I'll let you take all day to die. I've seen fellers gut-shot before, and some of 'em hung on for hours. Towards the end, they was beggin' for somebody to put 'em outta their misery. I reckon a belly wound is about the most painful of all. No way you can drink water, no matter how thirsty you git."

"Go to hell," he muttered thickly. "I ain't got nuthin' more to say to you, 'cep'n to leave me be."

"Fair enough," I told him as I got to my feet, with both guns in my hands. The Winchester he'd used was my own, given to me by my boss when we'd taken that herd up to Abilene town, fighting Indians and outlaws all the way. I was sure glad to get it back. You can bet your boots on that!

Walking over to where the fire was still smoldering, with my coffeepot in the coals, I found my saddle and blankets. Rolling up my camp bed, I tied it in back of the cantle. Not a sign of my saddlebags did I see, and that made me madder'n hell. What little money I'd had left was in those bags. It might pay to search through the wounded man's pockets, as he could well have had half the money on him. I figgered to do it before I buried him. No matter what I'd told him, there was no way I could leave any man dying and unburied.

Picking up my saddle and blanket, I headed for the trees where my bay horse was tied. I was wondering if he'd still remember me, when a scream from the wounded man caused me to spin around and drop the saddle on the ground. His screams continued like somebody was poking him with sharp knives, a sound no man likes to hear.

He screamed again and pointed up toward the sky, where two buzzards swung in circling flight. "Git 'em away! I'll tell you anythin' you wanna know. Jist keep 'em off of me!"

He covered his face with bloody hands, blubbering in terror. "Please, promise you'll bury me deep so's them birds can't pick at me! I'm sorry for what I done, honest to God! It was Donelson's idea. C'mere, mister. I got somethin' to say before I die. You gotta listen to me!"

I reckon no man knows how he'll react to dying. This man was a coward and a murderer, but I couldn't just ignore his pleading, no matter what he'd done. It just wasn't in me to deny him some comfort. Besides, he might tell me where his partner had gone and whether he had been waiting there for him to come back. I squatted down and told him I'd listen.

"Name's Braunt," he told me. "Stephen Braunt. I come on out here from Illinois after the war and worked as a miner for a spell. Got drunk one night in Hillsboro and woke up the next morning at Fort McRae. I'd let some sergeant talk me into enlistin' in the cavalry, the Sixth Cavalry, it was. At first I was purty mad, but I got over it. I ain't one to carry a grudge, and the Army's not so bad. I'd spent almost three years in the artillery durin' the war, and I'd had some good times, made some good friends. I almost—'' A fit of coughing shook him, and blood trickled from his nose and mouth. After a moment, he recovered and looked up at me. ''I'm a sure enough goner, ain't I? My legs; there's no feelin' in 'em. My back mus' be busted. I should've known when we run off from that stockade—'' He grimaced.

''Damn! I wish I could have some water. My gut's burnin' somethin' fierce! There's a canteen over by the fire. I'm gonna die, anyway, so what's the harm in givin' me a drink?''

He was right. What *was* the harm? I told him I'd bring a drink to him, and not to worry about the buzzards. With him still living, I doubted they'd come any closer. ''I'll bring you the canteen,'' I said. ''Mebbe a drink *would* help some.''

When I came back with the water, he'd emptied his pockets out on the ground beside him. My razor was there, case and all, along with my jackknife, which I'd forgotten about. My tobacco pouch and papers were in his hand, and he asked if I would mind rolling him a smoke. ''Prob'ly be the last one I ever have,'' he said, tears rolling down his stubbled cheeks.

Now, this man was a cold-blooded killer, and some folks'd wonder why I was paying him any mind, bringing him a canteen of water and bothering to roll him a cigarette. Well sir, I ain't never been one to kick a man when he's down, and it just wasn't in me to treat this feller any differently. I'd rolled the cigarette by then, lit it, and passed it over.

''What about my money?'' I asked. ''I had me some cash hid away in my saddlebags. Whatever happened to it?''

''Oh, yeah,'' he replied. ''I fergot about that! I got the most of it right here.'' Awkwardly, he reached into a pocket and brought out some coins: three double eagles and one five-dollar gold piece, along with some silver. Totaled up it came to more'n sixty-six dollars.

"Donelson only took ten bucks," he said. "After all, the money he'll get for the machinery will come to much more. I wanted to be sure I didn't wind up broke in case he fergets where to find me. You can un'erstan' that, can't you?"

"Then he *is* comin' back?" I asked. "You *were* waitin' for him here? What was he plannin' to do with my wagon?" As I asked the question, I had already figured out the answer, an answer that might mean much more'n a wagon and team to me!

He looked up, then turned his eyes away. "He'd planned to sell the whole kaboodle," he told me, "then buy a saddle horse. That way, he could come right across them mountains and not have to foller the canyons." He paused, struck by a fit of coughing and struggling to catch his breath. Bleeding badly from his nose and mouth, he grabbed my hand and tried to pull me in closer, his face a mask of panic.

"You promised me! Stay here until I'm gone! Bury me in under some rocks so's the varmints can't git at me. Please don't let me down, mister. I don't wanna die alone! You . . . you . . . I'm . . ." His hand opened, and his arm dropped to the ground limply. Chest heaving, he was struggling to breathe past the torrent of blood pouring from his mouth. I had to turn away. He'd sure enough gotten what he deserved, but no man wants to watch anybody die. Not like that!

A groping hand caught at my ankle, and I looked down. He was trying hard to say something, and so I bent over. His eyes bulged out and his face was contorted as he tried to raise himself on his elbows. "You . . . careful . . ." he gasped. "He kilt sargint . . . bare han's. Crazy . . . I . . . we . . . robbed. Caught us . . . we got away . . ." His back arched convulsively, his grip on my ankle loosened, and he sagged backward, eyes staring sightlessly at the sky, at the two birds wheeling in endless, searching patterns. Two black birds, with just a tinge of white on the trailing edges of their wings, heads red-wattled and naked of feathers. I shuddered and turned away. They were sure ugly critters, but they were borned to a purpose, like everything else on God's earth. I had killed men before but would never get used to it.

CHAPTER 10

T HAT SORREL STUD WAS THE STRONGEST OF THE TWO horses, and even he had to struggle up the shale-strewn slopes. Hard as it had been to descend, it was even more difficult to climb. Tied on behind were my bay and the pack mule, and their efforts to hold back made the going mighty tough. I was leaning as far over the stud's withers as I could, trying to assist in the scramble for footing but not helping much. Finally, as we came to a particularly rough spot, I slid off and walked up the slope, pulling the string with me. I was remembering the words I'd heard from Braunt and was desperate to reach that water hole where Nell and Pop had promised to wait.

I'd buried Braunt in the Apache manner, dropping his body down into a deep crevice and caving rocks over him. It was a cinch no animal could ever get to him, and that was all he had asked. It might not have been the burial he'd wanted to have, but my conscience was clear. I'd notify the Army, and they could dig him out of there if they wanted him all that badly. I'd left a crude cross as a marker.

Taken us the better part of two hours to reach the top of the mesa. I'd filled both canteens from the little creek in the canyon and used some to rinse out the mouths of my animals. It didn't take care of their thirst, but it helped cool them down. I allowed myself only a swallow. Once we'd gotten that done, I stepped onto the sorrel and headed on over to where I'd last seen Nell and the old Indian. I couldn't help but worry. The way Braunt had talked, there was a good chance that his partner, Donelson, might pass close by to the water hole, or the *tinaja*, as Pop had called it. In truth, the word '*tinaja*' means a large earthen jar in Spanish, but in the territories it was used to describe pockets in the rocks that trapped water during the infrequent rains. Water that could mean the difference between life and death to any-body, Indians or whites, who traveled the southwestern deserts.

If troopers from Fort McRae used this particular *tinaja*, Don-elson might well know about it and count on watering his horse before beginning the descent into the canyon. My two compan-ions were unarmed except for Pop's lance, since I was carrying the only gun we owned. They'd have no defense.

Riding out onto the point where we'd parted company with one another, I shaded my eyes and stared down at the pool of water that was plainly visible in the clear mountain air. No signs of occu-pancy could be seen: no thin tendril of smoke from a hat-sized fire, no horses feeding on the sparse graze. The little spot of blue and green seemed as empty as last year's promises of rain.

Looking down at the ground, I could see the scuffed rocks and gouged dirt where they'd made their descent, sliding on horses' hind ends as they rode their way to the bottom. So all this wasn't no dream. My Nell and that old Indian *had* headed for the water hole! Now it looked as if they'd been snatched off the earth or swallowed up by some big hole in the ground. Once more, I stared down at the pool, trying to *will* them to be there. But nary a sign of life did I see.

Both Winchesters were hanging by thongs from the saddle's wide, flat horn. I checked them, making certain live rounds were in their chambers. Then, hefting one in my right hand, I gigged the sorrel and started the sliding descent toward the bottom of the slope, holding the carbine across the bows of the saddle. Fear of what I might find made me reckless, and I dug my moccasined heels into the sorrel's flanks, making him squeal in anger. Reaching with his thick neck bowed and his lips peeled back from big, yellow teeth, he snapped viciously at my foot, missing by a fraction. My fist came down between his ears with a thud, and he stumbled and almost fell but then caught himself in time.

"I ain't blamin' you none," I hollered, "but this time is different. I'm in a hurry, and you'd best rattle your hocks down this here slide, or I'll sure enough make you harder'n heck to ketch! Now, c'mon, hoss. Git to gittin'!"

Behind us, my bay gelding and the mule had squatted down on their haunches, forefeet braced, and were sliding toward the bottom of the slope in a shower of stones. I let them go on their own, flinging away the lead rope so they'd be free to choose. Reared back on the sorrel's rump, I bounced and bumped and clung on tight, feet shoved deep in the iron stirrups. It was a wild ride, but we made it down safely, a bit the worse for wear but still in one piece.

Once down on the flat, I hazed the two loose animals and grabbed up the lead rope, then headed toward the *tinaja* at a flat-out run. Reins and lead rope in one hand and cocked rifle in the other, I raced toward the clump of trees, hoping I was wrong but fearful of what I might find.

Suddenly Buck burst out of the thicket, almost under the stud's nose, and the big horse reared, pawing at the sky. I hit the ground with a thump, and the gun went off, practically in my ear. I sat there feeling foolish as the sorrel buck-jumped on tightly bunched feet, headed toward the pool of water. The dog was all over me, licking my face, letting me know how glad he was to see me. Nell ran out, with Pop a close second, and joined in the melee.

Falling to her knees, she throwed her arms around me and kissed me full on the mouth, squeezing me tight until I had to holler for help. "Hey!" I cried. "Give a feller room to breathe, will you. I ain't been gone all thet long."

The old man was patting me on the back and mumbling some sort of greeting with a big grin on his wrinkled old face. They helped me to my feet and brushed off some of the sand and twigs, all the time telling me how glad they were to see me. I put an arm around Nell's shoulders and hugged her.

"Honey," I said, "you ain't got no idea how scared I was. I figgered thet feller with the gold tooth had been here. I was imaginin' all sorts of scary things and thinkin' worse. Talkin' about thet . . ." I looked around and saw the sorrel, the bay, and the pack mule drinking from the pond.

"We'd best ketch up them critters and git 'em back where they can't be seen. Thet feller could be showin' up here at any time, and we sure as heck don't want to scare him off."

Nell put her hand on my arm and looked up. "How can you be sure he's coming?" she asked. "What did you find in that canyon, Jake? Whose horse is that? Whose mule? Where were they, in that canyon? Did you see the killers? Find tracks made by the wagon? Please, Jake. Answer me!"

"I'll tell you all about it," I replied. "But first we have to git them horses out of sight. C'mon, Pop! You give me a hand with 'em, will you. Then I'll tell you the whole story. I promise! Nell, git thet dog outta sight, quick!"

The big stud wasn't all that anxious to be caught, but we got him cornered, and I grabbed at the headstall. Soon's he felt my hand on him, he calmed right down. After climbing a mighty steep rise and fighting that treacherous footing, he was still full of vinegar, ready to ride if I needed him. I told him what a good horse he was and how I was figgering to give him a big feed of grain whenever we got to where it could be had. I rubbed him all over so's he'd get used to my scent and not spook if I had to come up on him unexpectedly, like after dark. He was a fine animal, and I well understood why Nell's husband had treasured him.

If we ever had our wish come true and settled on a place of our own, he'd make a great sire, and we could expect some really good colts from him. Even a grade mare would throw a quality colt if he was the sire. I bent over and lifted a forefoot. The hoof was rock-hard and well rounded, with an open heel. He showed no signs of ever having been shod, but I was sure that he'd worn rawhide boots a time or two. I'd sorta lost track of where I was, when I felt a gentle pinch on my rear. Not a bite but just a nibble, a reminder so I would respect him and know what he *could* do. I grinned and rubbed my hind end. With no seat in the leggings, there wasn't much back there to protect me, just the breechcloth. He had teeth like chisels, as all horses do, and I knew how much it could hurt from experience.

We picketed the animals on a bit of graze, a small clearing Nell and Pop had found back of a tangle of trees. They were eager to hear what I'd found and pestered me for the story, so we all sat down by the fire, and I started telling them about the man in the canyon.

"He was the one who killed your husband," I told her. "I gave him a fair shake, even though I could have put a bullet into him from ambush, like he'd have done had it been turnabout. I had a fair bead on him from behind some rocks but couldn't bring myself to pull the trigger. He was jest sittin' there by a fire, waitin' for the coffee to boil, when I shot the pot off a rock and told him to stand up. He tried to shoot it out, grazed my shoulder as a matter of fact, but it don't hurt none." I hastened to reassure Nell, who had fixed an eye on my bloodstained hunting shirt.

"You might put some of thet salve of yours on it if you git a chance," I told her. "Right now, let me finish what I got to say, 'cause it's important.

"Anyways, he was a medium-sized hombre and didn't have a beard nor a gold tooth like the feller who beat me, so I reckon he fits the description of your husband's killer. He didn't deny doin' it, but he did put most of the blame agin his partner, man name of Donelson. Said Donelson forced him to do what he did. Also said Donelson was crazy and mumbled somethin' about Donelson killin' a sergeant with his bare hands. He warned me to be mighty careful around Donelson.

"Bein' gut-shot, it taken him a while to go, and thet's no good. When he found out he was gonna die there, he whimpered and cried whilst he was bleedin' out. A couple of them old turkey buzzards flew over and circled around. Thet was when he busted down and commenced cryin' and beggin' me to stick by him until he passed on. Oh, yeah. Them britches! The ones you found, Pop. They was his, and he was wearin' a pair of mine, along with my boots and brush jacket. Braunt. Thet was his name, same as the one on the death warrant. He made me promise to bury him deep so's the varmints couldn't git at him, and thet's what I done.

Dropped him down in one of them big cracks in the rocks and piled a passel of rocks down on top of his body.

"Jest before he died, he told me thet Donelson planned to sell my wagon and team. Then he was gonna buy a horse and come back over the mountain. Thet's why I came down in such an all-fired hurry. There's a chance he jest might be headed this way, figgerin' to water here at the hole. We'd best be ready for him when he shows up, don't you reckon?"

Pop sputtered out a whole bunch of Apache words, and Nell kept nodding her head. "He wants one of the rifles so that he can go stand guard," she told me. "I'd better fix up the wound in your shoulder, Jake. Even a scratch can cause some trouble later on. Give him my rifle and then take off the shirt. Please, Jake. Do as I say if you really care."

I forked over the rifle and some extra cartridges. That old man's eyes lit up prideful-like, and he slipped through the trees and out of sight in less time than it takes for a man to say howdy. I skinned out of the shirt and handed it over to Nell, who was waiting with a little pot in her hand.

I sat down again, and she bent over me, her sweet scent and her nearness making my blood race through my veins. The thought of her belonging to me someday soon was uppermost in my mind or I would have grabbed her right then. With a light touch, she explored the bloody groove left by Braunt's bullet, washing it with a dampened cloth and gently rubbing in her cure-all salve.

"What's in thet stuff?" I asked. "Whatever it's made out of, it sure enough did a good job on the last of my scrapes and bruises. They healed up in no time at all."

She looked up at me, grinning, her face mischievous and child-like. "If I told you," she said, "then you wouldn't be back for more treatment. I'd lose a patient, and I wouldn't like that. Would you?"

"No, ma'am," I replied. "Right now, I feel like I've done died and gone straight to heaven. Now that you've had plenty of time to think it over, have you considered what I asked you a few days back? Will you marry me, Nell?"

She stepped back and looked me over sorta serious-like. "Well, I don't know, Jake. You only have the one horse and that mule. Remember, my grandmother's bride price was much

more. Twenty horses! Then, of course, the rifle and a keg of
rum. You have only one rifle and no rum at all. Maybe you
could part with the mule, but you must have a horse, and your
rifle is your only protection. Would you consider this a bargain
if you were in my place? Would you respect me as a one-horse
bride, so to speak? No, I think we should stay with traditions
and let our courtship, if it is ever really to materialize, be followed according to that same tradition of value.'' She giggled.
''Don't look so shocked, Jake, as if I'm turning down your pro-
posal. In a way I'm accepting, with a few conditions, of course.''

About then was when I made a mistake, one that came very
close to separating us permanently. I knew I was wrong as soon
as the words left my lips, but being thickheaded and just plain
dumb, I went ahead and spoke them.

''But,'' I said, ''how about the little feller? Ain't folks gonna
wonder about the baby, us not bein' man and wife? You don't
mind havin' him called a bad name for not havin' a father?''

Nell stiffened and stepped back a pace. Her face set in stony
lines, she looked at me like I'd just crawled out from under a
rock somewheres. For a long moment she said nothing, and
realizing I'd made a terrible mistake, I was trying to find words
to explain what I'd meant. It was too late!

''My baby has a father,'' she told me. ''His father was one of
the bravest men I've ever known. He was murdered by men like
you. White men! Men who lie and cheat my people with no
sense of doing wrong. Men who think of us as savages, to be
treated like animals. We are human beings. We know love and
hate, just as you do, just as any human being would know them.
We ask only to be left alone, to be allowed to live a life as we have
known it for generations on our land. The lands we have lived on
for hundreds of years! To live as we want to live, hunting for our
food or growing it. We left the reservation because they herd us
like animals and treat us like we are dirt under their feet!

''Go from this place,'' she told me. ''You are healed now,
and you have no further need of us. Take your horse. Leave me
alone and never come near me, ever again! You are no better
than the rest, and I hate you, just as I hate all the whites! I hate
you! Do you hear me? I hate you!''

CHAPTER 11

〰〰〰

THERE WASN'T MUCH I COULD SAY OR DO AFTER that. I saddled my bay horse after he and the mule had both drunk from the pool. Pop came out from wherever he'd been and watched in silence, knowing that something was wrong but unable to do anything about it. Buck came over just as I put my foot in the stirrup and whined, reaching out with a paw, wanting to be petted, I reckon. I swung up and sat there a moment, my head full of unspoken words and my heart aching for want of her. She had turned away so I couldn't see her face, but I was sure she was crying silently. I hadn't meant the words to mean anything wrong, but she'd taken them that way. Now it was all over! I'd hurt her, and hurt her badly. Nothing I could say would undo the wrong. It was time to leave, before I made a complete damn fool of myself.

I jerked the bay's head around and slammed my heels into his flanks. Startled, he reared up, and his head smacked me on the nose, bringing the blood in a hurry. Not wanting her to see what'd happened, I heeled him again, and he broke into a fast lope, with the mule trotting behind.

Soon's we were out of sight, I brought him up short, wiped
my nose with the back of my hand, and felt of it tenderly. It
wasn't broken, and that was a pure blessing. I sure didn't need
any more hurts, not now! The bleeding stopped a moment later,
and I washed my hands and face with water from the canteen. It
still smarted, but that would go away soon.

I'd headed in the general direction of Red Rock, the town
Nell had mentioned as a possible destination for the killers. I
was still concerned about Donelson watering at the *tinaja* but
figured I'd intercept him before he could reach there. It was
coming on to sunset, and soon it would be too dark to travel. I'd
have to make a dry camp somewhere, and soon. Not only a dry
camp but a hungry one! I had been in such an all-fired hurry to
leave, I'd run off without any of the jerked beef we'd worked so
hard to prepare.

The going was fairly easy, just a gentle downslope, which although rocky wasn't loose shale, like the one I'd traversed
earlier that day. What I was looking for was a hollow or swale,
somewhere we'd have a little protection from the wind and chill
that came with desert nights. So far I'd had no luck, but a mile
or so ahead I could see what looked like a dip in the terrain.
We'd been on the move for two hours at least and were more'n
six miles from where Pop and Nell had their camp. So far I'd
seen no signs of tracks, except for those of deer and javelina.
The slope was so bare, I would have spotted Donelson if he had
been anywhere nearby. Suddenly I saw smoke rising in a thin,
straight line, coming out of that depression I'd noticed earlier.

Now that I was closer, I could also see a few trees, with their
tops about even with the ground. There must be a valley, I
thought to myself, rather than just a shallow arroyo. It was
going to be darned tough for me to get in very close without
being spotted, and I felt sort of naked out there in the open. Dismounting, I brought the mule up close so that I could walk between the two animals. This way, I had a bit of cover from
Donelson's bullets if he *was* there. Not much cover, but enough
so's I might get off a shot or two before he nailed me. Closer
now, I could smell the smoke and also the scent of frying

bacon. My belly rumbled, and I cursed the bunch of dumb words that had left me in this predicament.

A horse whistled off in the trees, and the bay answered before I could clamp my hand on his nose. My mule joined in with a long bray and tried to pull ahead, so for a moment I had my hands full trying to keep them from running off.

Then I heard the clatter of horses' hooves and looked up at four soldiers coming right toward me at a dead run. A loud hail, unmistakable in its intent, stopped me cold.

"Just hold it right there, Injun! We got you dead in our sights, so don't you move. Drop that rifle, and I mean now! Stay right where you are." All four had carbines pointed at me, and their faces weren't exactly what I'd call friendly.

"For gosh sakes, fellers," I hollered. "Don't shoot! I'm a white man."

"You're a what?" he asked. "Don't look like no white man to me with all them Injun trappings. You just keep still a minute till I kin look you over, mister." He shoved close and peered down at me.

"Well I'll be double-dee-damned," he exclaimed. "You are a white man. What in hell you doin' out here dressed up in them Injun duds? You lost or sump'n? You're damn lucky we didn't just shoot you and pick at your carcass afterwards."

"Are you the boss man here?" I asked him. "If you are, I got somethin' to say thet jest might interest you."

"Nope," he replied. "I'm just in command of these three dummies. You'll have to talk to the lieutenant if'n you got somethin' impo'tant. Hop up on that horse of your'n, and we will escort you into camp. You keep that rifle pointed away from me, y'hear, mister. Point it down to the ground until we get where we're goin'. I'll lead out," he told the other men, "and you all foller in behind. Keep your eyes on him!"

The lieutenant turned out to be a tired-looking man with silver bars on his shoulders and disillusionment in his appearance. He was gray-haired and could have been somewhere near forty, a mite old for his rank. Sprawled about a fire were eight more soldiers, black like the ones who'd caught me. They didn't bother to rise when we rode in but stared at me and my

Indian outfit. I'd seen that lieutenant once before and was hoping he wouldn't remember me.

Dismounting, the corporal tossed off a casual salute, and the officer returned it just as haphazardly. "Found him on the trail," the corporal said. "Figured he was an Injun in them buckskin clothes, but it turns out he's a white man."

The officer rose from his campstool and brushed off what passed for a uniform: a loose fatigue blouse that he wore outside a pair of slick cowhide pants; scuffed, run over at the heels boots with blunt spurs; an oversized yellow bandanna knotted around a corded, muscular neck; and a battered slouch hat that had seen better days. As I stepped off the bay, I noticed he was a couple inches taller'n me and somewhat thicker in the middle, where a .44 Army Colt hung butt forward in a regulation holster. He looked me over with a frown on his deeply lined face and thrust out his hand.

"Waggonier," he said. "Rufus M. First lieutenant of the Ninth U.S. Cavalry out of Fort Bayard. Your face is familiar to me, but I don't recall the circumstances."

"Name's Jake Bailey," I told him as we shook hands. "It was about two years back, Lieutenant, mebbe a mite more. Me and some other boys had a run-in with a land-grabbin' Yankee who was treatin' our boss mighty shameful. That was over by Atascosa, down South Texas way, and you 'n' your outfit chased us halfway 'cross Bexar County. Near caught us once, and I sort of jostled you off your horse in gittin' away. I hope you ain't still sore about thet, Lieutenant. Didn't mean no harm, honest. It was jest thet I didn't have no time to explain, and you prob'ly wouldn't have listened, anyways."

A half smile spread across his face, and he nodded. "You needn't worry, Bailey. As it turned out, the man you roughed up was a wanted criminal. He went to prison, and the old man you helped got his land back. Sit down." He waved his hand toward the stool. "I had just sent the corporal on an errand, and he intercepted you on his way out of the canyon. My sergeant has another detail of men scouting for two prisoners who escaped from Fort McRae. We almost caught one of them yesterday. He headed south, so the sergeant's on what amounts to a wild goose chase. Excuse me for a moment."

He turned away and spoke to the hulking corporal, waving his hands and pointing toward the northeast. Sitting down was the last thing I wanted to do right then. My belly was still growling, and the thick slices of bacon I could see in the two big skillets over the fire made my mouth water. "I don't s'pose you boys could spare a couple pieces of bacon," I asked. "To be honest, my belly thinks my throat's cut. I ain't had no eats since early mornin', and I'd sure like to do somethin' about it. I could use some of the coffee, too, if you got enough to go around."

A mustachioed trooper handed me a tin plate, along with a cup and fork. "He'p yo'se'f," he told me with a grin. "I sure do like thet outfit," he went on. "I see'd me a feller once't who looked jist like you. Was over to Fo't Kearney, and he was some kinda mount'in man, they said. Made hisse'f some big money trappin' animals fer their hides. Had him a Injun wife, too, all dressed up in beads 'n' buckskin. Mighty ugly, she was, but he seemed to like her fine. She sure was fat, thet lady! 'Bout as fat as I ever did see! He he he! I kin see her jigglin' now. She jiggled all over!"

I joined in the laugh with the others as I spread some bacon out of one skillet. Pouring myself a cup of coffee, I hunkered down nearby and began eating, watching while the corporal mounted and led the way out of the canyon. The lieutenant came back to the fire and filled his cup before resuming his seat on the stool.

"The corporal tells me you have some information for me," he said. "I'd appreciate hearing it, but go ahead and eat a bite first." He reached down into a saddlebag that leaned against the stool and brought out a silver flask. Removing the cap, he poured a healthy shot of liquor into his cup. I shook my head when he proffered the flask.

"No thanks, Lieutenant. I ain't had nothin' to drink for more'n a month. Whiskey, that is. More'n likely it'd knock me for a loop, and I need to keep my head on straight. Give me a minute to eat this grub, and I'll tell you all I know."

As I squatted there, I could hear whispers and more giggling from the others. Out of the corner of an eye, I saw a coin change hands, and all eight men were grinning broadly.

"Say, Mister Bailey." It was the trooper who'd handed me the utensils. He cleared his throat and began again.

"Uh, Mister Bailey! Has you got a seat in them pants of your'n, or is thet yo' bare bottom under thet blue cloth? Don't mean no disrespect, mind yuh. We jist cu'ious, thet's all. No disrespect," he said again, still grinning.

I finished chewing and then swallowed noisily. Laying aside the plate and fork, I took a long drink of coffee and looked him square in the eyes. He wiggled uncomfortably, and a look of dismay replaced the grin. He turned away.

"Bare bottom," I told him, and laughed at his reaction.

"See!" he hollered. "I tol' you so. Gimme my dollar!"

"Where on earth did you find that costume?" The lieutenant's question caught me off guard. The last thing I wanted to do was tell him about Nell and the old man. He'd be sure to send men out after them, and if they were caught, it was a gut cinch they'd be sent back to the reservation, that is, if they were lucky. Some Apaches were being shipped all the way to Florida and kept in an old Spanish fort. If she was to survive, I'd have to stretch the truth just a mite.

I fumbled for my pipe and realized I didn't have it. My hunting shirt had no pockets, come to find out, and the pipe was back at Nell's camp. The lieutenant shook his head, but the trooper with the mustache came to my rescue again.

"Heah you be, Mister Bailey." He handed me a pouch with tobacco and papers. After I rolled a smoke, I gave him back his pouch and lit up with a splinter from the fire.

I explained to the lieutenant about being beaten with the chain and waking up to find my wagon, my team, and all that I owned stolen. "Taken every stitch of clothes I had 'cep'n for my underdrawers. Only saw the one man, the one who used the trace chain on me. A big man, he was, with a full black beard and a single gold tooth in his lower jaw. I know now that his name was Donelson, and I reckon he's one of the two men you've been huntin'. Ain't I right, Lieutenant?"

Waggonier nodded and leaned closer. "Start again at the be-ginning. You say you were on your way to Lordsburg?"

"Thet's right, Lieutenant. I had a contract to haul some ma-chinery down to a copper mine near Lordsburg. I taken my time along the way, because I weren't in no big hurry. I'd worked a cattle drive to Colorado and figgered a little bit of rest never hurt nobody, and I'd sure earned my share!

"Anyways, them two jumped me in the middle of the night and near beat me to death. A dog woke me up the next mornin', lickin' my face and tryin' to git me off the ground in one piece. Mighty nice dog, Lieutenant, saved my life!"

I went on to tell about dragging myself to the creek and how I'd lain there in the warm water. How I came to find my axe and built a shelter. How I'd made up the travois so's I could haul the wood and how I'd wound up tying my body to the travois with strips of cloth from my underdrawers. How I'd woke up and found myself among a flock of Indians. The word "flock" came easy to me somehow. If I was going to be a liar, I figured I might as well make my lie a big one.

"Who were they, man?" he asked. "Do you have any idea of the tribe or where they came from? It's very important."

I shook my head. "Nope. I think they was Apaches, but I couldn't say for sure. Mostly they talked in Injun, except for one younger one who talked pretty good American.

"They patched me up and fed me good. Soon as I'd healed up enough, one lady made me this outfit. Reckon they didn't care much for my underdrawers." I laughed, but I was watch-ing him from under lowered lids. He seemed to believe what I was telling him.

"You said you knew one man was named Donelson. How could you possibly find that out? You're right, incidentally. They *are* the ones we're searching for. But continue, please. We need to know all you can tell us. Go on, if you will."

"Well, sir, I'll try to make this as short as I can. Thet bunch of Injuns was trackin' them two men same as you are. Seems one of their men was beaten to death by them. They'd snuck up on the Injuns' camp whilst the men was out huntin' for meat. All thet was left in camp was one woman, an older feller, and a

man who was sick or sump'n. Them two attacked the sick man
and beat his head in with a club. Accordin' to the woman, they
was both barefoot and wearin' ragged clothes. She taken a rifle
and chased 'em off. Reckon the dog runned after them and
come to find me instead. Injuns don't really git mad, you know;
they git even. That's why I was treated the way I was, or leastways I reckoned so. I'd showed guts in doin' what I did, and
they admire that. I'd never done them no harm, so they had no
call to hurt me.'' I shrugged. ''I got no other explanation, Lieutenant.

''Soon as I could sit a horse, we moved out. When we come
to where I'd made camp, one of them Injuns found some pants,
ragged Army pants thet one of them fellers had tossed out after
he got some of my good ones to wear. In the pocket I found a
death warrant. The name on it was Stephen Braunt.

''Right away, them Injuns wanted to take out after 'em. I
convinced them we should split up, let one bunch foller down
the left branch of the canyon, and the other take the right. The
Injuns argued some, seein' as how they was sure them two
turned south. Finally, they gave me a rifle and picked one man
to go along with me and check out thet right branch. I reckon he
was sure he was gonna miss all the fun. I know he acted mad at
me for havin' to tag along on what he figgered was a wild goose
chase. He kept hangin' back, and we hadn't gone more'n two
miles when he disappeared, jest faded plumb outta sight! Not
thet I cared much, you understand.

''About the time I was ready to give up and try to foller him,
I seen some smoke. Jest a mite of smoke, but enough to let me
know there was somebody down there, somebody thet was too
dumb to make a fire thet wouldn't give him away. Ain't no Injun nor no Western man thet can't do thet. Had to be some
dumb soldier. Uh . . . 'scuse me, Lieutenant. I didn't mean
thet jest like it sounded.

''Once I got close enough, I tied up my horse and injuned
down the canyon till I got to where I could see him. Mebbe
sixty, seventy feet away. First off, I figgered to jest kill him.
You know, jest shoot him without givin' no warnin' at all. Matter of fact, I drew down on him, but when I come to pullin' the

trigger, I jest couldn't do it. Ain't my style, I reckon. Anyways, I decided to call him out and fight him fair. Give him the chance that he never gave me. I s'pose you figger me for a fool, but thet's how I do things.''

Here, Waggonier interrupted me. "But," he said, "you'd never seen him before. You told me that. How could you be sure it was Braunt? Donelson you had seen, or at least were able to describe to a point. He does have a beard and one gold tooth. Both are listed in his description. How could you recognize Braunt, never having seen him?''

I shrugged. "Well, sir, the man had tied my saddle horse and pack mule close by. He was wearin' my brush jacket and a hat I bought in Abilene two years back. If you want to unroll that Injun blanket behind my cantle, you'll find all of my personal gear. My razor, my jackknife, and—" I suddenly remembered—my tobacco pouch! I had rolled the pouch in the blanket. Having gotten used to a pipe, I'd forgotten to leave the pouch where I could use it. I told Waggonier, and he agreed to wait while I got out my makin's.

Once I'd rolled another smoke, I went on with my story, a good bit of which was the truth. How I had been forced into killing Braunt when he shot at me. "I figgered to give him an even break," I said. "You know, both of us startin' with rifles down by our sides. He snuck in a shot and grazed my shoulder. He never had time for a second. Shot through the guts, it taken him a while to die. He told me all about his partner. Said it was mostly his fault, the partner's, or so he told me. He was waitin' there for Donelson to come back to the canyon, and then they'd head for Old Mexico. I guess I never will see thet wagon again. It's long gone by now.''

Waggonier smiled. "Oh, but you're wrong, Bailey. Your wagon is safe at Fort Bayard, with the contents intact. You can go there and claim it any time you wish.''

I reckon my mouth must have been hanging open, because he laughed and then explained about the wagon. I didn't quite know what to say. I'd really figured my wagon was gone and didn't think I'd ever see it again. The lieutenant went on, but he was no longer laughing. Shoulders slumped, he hunched over on the stool and stared at the ground.

"You will remember me telling you about our near capture of one of the fugitives? It was yesterday, as I said, and a two-man scouting party came across the wagon. It was hidden in a clearing about a mile north of Silver City. When they approached to investigate, Donelson fired on them. His shot killed one trooper, knocked him from his saddle and down to the ground. Before the other man could return the fire, another shot from Donelson struck him in the shoulder. He was badly wounded but managed to stay conscious long enough to reach our position.

"I mounted the troop, and we raced to intercept Donelson before he could escape. We were too late. From the sign in the clearing, we determined that he had caught up the trooper's horse and had fled toward the south. We were able to use the wagon to transport the wounded man back to the fort, as well as the body of the dead man. There's no doubt about the ambusher being Donelson. The wounded trooper got a good look at him before he was hit."

I shook my head. "What are you doin' *here*, Lieutenant? Why ain't you all chasin' thet killer 'stead of sittin' out here on your rears? I don't understand you people. You've never done nothin' right as far's I see. You mark my word! Thet killin' son is gonna git away clean, and you ain't makin' a move to stop him. Ain't none of yuh would make a pimple on a real soldier's butt. You're worse'n nothin'!"

"That's enough, *Mister* Bailey!" Waggonier wasn't slumped over, not now. He was on his feet and glaring at me. "You shut your mouth, you hear me! I've sat here, and I listened to your little tale of woe. Listened with sympathy and let part of what you were saying go in one ear and out the other. Do you think for one minute that I believed the Apaches had nursed you, fed you, clothed you, and then gave you a rifle and let you go wandering off? Do you actually think I could believe a cock-and-bull story like that? Apaches aren't in love with us; they hate us! Don't take me for a fool. What brought you to this godforsaken place? Cattle are few and far between around here.

Mining! That's the current craziness. Gives us cause for nothing but grief. Drunken scuts bedevil the Indians, chase after their women, and treat them like animals. Is it any wonder the Apaches are killing and stealing everything in sight? We're caught in the middle of all this mess, trying to put down the Apaches so we can take care of the few who no longer want to fight. You story is so full of holes, it could pass for a lace doily on my mother's favorite chair. Now, you sit there and listen to me, or I'll have you bound and gagged!"

He paced around, pounding a fist into his palm. "Where is the horse the Indians let you have? If you recovered the rifle that was stolen, why don't I see two of them? How can you expect me to believe any part of your story? Why should I? Tell me that." He sat down on the campstool and tore at his collar with shaking hands. He was sure enough mad, and I couldn't really blame him.

"We'll get Donelson. You can be sure of that, Bailey. I am only waiting for the rest of my men to rejoin us. Like a fool, I let the sergeant talk me into splitting up my force, but he'll be back, and soon. Then we will be off after the deserter, and you'll be going with us. You can forget about your precious wagon! Chances are, you may not even get back alive if I have my way. I'm going to put you out in front, where you can have your try at killing Donelson before he's able to get you. For all I know, you may be part and parcel of the escape from Fort McRae. Those men were being heavily guarded and could never have broken out without some help. You may consider yourself under arrest, that is, unless your memory has improved and you have some more to tell me."

He had me dead to rights, and I couldn't even feel mad at him. I'd pegged him all wrong, I could see that, but I sure didn't know how to square myself with him without I quit my lying. But first I had to have a real convincing argument.

Three quick steps put me right alongside the bay and my Winchester rifle. "Lieutenant," I said as I eared the hammer back to full cock, "you're one hundred percent right in most everythin' you've said. I did stretch the truth somewhat, but I had me a good reason. First off, I wasn't mixed up in no escape, and I sure as heck ain't tryin' to help old Donelson git away. All you'd have to do is see the scars on me, scars left by thet trace chain, the one he used to near beat me to death. I killed Braunt because he had it comin' to him, but I gave him a fair shake. Now, you jest sit down on thet stool, and you listen! The rest of you—'' I motioned with the rifle. ''Keep your hands where I can see 'em or I'll shoot your ears off!

''What I said about them two killin' an Indian was a fact. They did sneak into an Indian camp and club a man to death. But there wasn't a whole batch of Indians like I said. As a matter of fact, there were jest two others: an old man in his seventies and a young woman who was big with child. A woman who taken me in, dressed my wounds, and treated me the same as if I were part of her family. She saved my life! I grew to love the* woman, and if she'd have me, I'd marry her in a minute. My trouble was not knowin' when to keep my big mouth shut! There's times for talkin' and times when you'd best leave things take their own natural course. I pushed her, said things I'd no right to say, and all because I just wanted her to say yes. Not later on, but right now!

''I didn't mean to hurt her feelin's, but I did. Them two killers beat her husband to death and did it right in front of her eyes. She needs time to decide what *she* wants from this world. I was too blinded with love to see it, but I do now.'' I shifted my grip on the rifle and rested it on my shoulder, muzzle pointing toward the sky. ''Don't try to backtrack me, Lieutenant, thinkin' you can find her and the old man. Not even a hound dog could pick up thet sign, with all its twistin' and turnin's, over solid rock. I figgered somebody might and was extra careful. Yep! They're just a couple of Apaches, and accordin' to your rules they'd broke the law when they jumped the reservation. The reservation! Where the white man's bounty keeps their bellies half filled with stringy range beef and breaks their hearts by takin' away their freedom. You think on thet!

''How about you?'' I pointed to the soldier who had loaned me his tobacco. ''It 'pears to me thet your folks were no better off than these Injuns. Somebody had to help them git their freedom or they'd still be slavin' away for white men and takin' whatever the white man wanted to hand out.''

He lowered his head and stirred the dirt with a toe. As he did, some of the others muttered to one another and moved around nervously. I carefully lowered the rifle's hammer a notch and hung the gun on my saddle horn, then turned to the lieutenant and spoke quietly.

"Now you know the whole story, Lieutenant. You'd best be makin' up your mind. Am I under arrest, or can I go over to the fort and claim my wagon? You don't have to worry about me usin' the rifle. I didn't have a live round in the chamber. I jest wanted to be sure you'd listen to my story, and I figgered thet was the best way to git your attention.''

Waggonier's smile was a thin one. "I wasn't worried," he said. "You see, I don't always play fair; in fact, I had an ace in the hole. Look over behind those rocks, Bailey, the ones to your right. You'll see two aces in the hole."

I did as he asked and saw two rifle muzzles dead aimed at my head. As I watched, two Apaches stood up, each with a big grin on his dark face. Both were holding Spencers, the carbine variety, seven-shot repeaters that chambered .56-56 cartridges. At that range, I would have been dead before I hit the ground!

CHAPTER 12

$\sim\!\!\times\!\!\sim$

As it turned out, Waggonier hadn't believed I
was involved with Braunt and Donelson, but he'd known I was
lying or at least leaving out part of my story. He just didn't want
me or anybody else to play him for a fool. For that I didn't
blame him, nor would anyone.

The two Apaches were his scouts. They'd been off on some
mission and had come back while I was doing all that talking.
He had seen them come in and motioned for them to remain out
of sight until he gave them a signal.

Waggonier and I were friendly again, and I was not under arrest. By that time it was too dark to go anywhere, so we sat back
from the fire and did some talking. He had served with the
Army during the late war and was, in fact, a true career officer.
He'd been with Grant's army and had climbed up to full colonel
before Lee's surrender. Like many of the brevetted officers, he
had dropped back to his permanent rank of second lieutenant
when the war was officially over.

"When these black regiments were formed," he told me,
"we were given a chance at command and promised rapid pro-

motion in rank if we volunteered to serve with them. It's easy to see how I've been rewarded." He touched his silver bars.

"I really shouldn't complain," he went on. "After all, we have just ten regiments of cavalry in the entire U.S. Army. The captains number only one hundred and twenty, as do first lieutenants. There are a mere thirty authorized majors, ten colonels, and ten brigadier generals. As you can well imagine, we wait like harpies for someone's death or retirement. I really don't mind the promotion list's inequities. Rarely does anyone gain promotion out of sequence. After all, I am still a young man and have many years ahead of me, that is, if I don't die of an Apache arrow or a drunken miner's gun. They hate us, you know. We interfere with progress. We are in the way, so to speak. If it were left to them, all these Indians would be shot on sight, the only 'good' Indian being a dead one, or so they say. Some few want Indians to live forever— the unscrupulous agents who rob and deceive them."

"Tell me," he asked. "What are your plans if you're able to persuade this lady to become your wife? Will you stay in the territory or go back to Texas? What will you do for a living? It's not easy, you know, unless you are thinking to become a miner. There's not much else for a white to do."

He had already told me that he had just celebrated his thirty-second year, something I found hard to believe. He really looked much older, and he blamed it on the life he'd lived as a professional soldier. "Here on the frontier," he said, "we are in the field much of the time. The rigors of a climate that ranges from burning heat to freezing cold raises hell with a man's health. Add to that the fact that we have not one qualified doctor in the field, and you might understand our situation. I myself have been wounded three times in just the past year. Granted, they were slight wounds, but I suffered just the same. Each time I had to content myself with treatment in the field, treatment by men who were not trained for medical services, common soldiers whose filthy hands had touched God knows what only moments before!

"Unless you are lucky enough to be very near a post, this is standard operating procedure, based on written orders. I have had to watch men die because we couldn't end a patrol merely to bring a wounded man to the post hospital. This is not something that seldom occurs; it is a horror we must put up with if we value our commissions. To disobey is evidence of cowardice and grounds for a general court-martial. The life of a soldier is a brutal and unhappy one that tears at your guts and makes you an old man before your time. Look around at these men. Some of them will be dead in less than a year's time. A fraction might make it to retirement, with twenty years needed to qualify. Can you imagine? Twenty of the most grueling years a man could withstand, and for what? Eighteen dollars per month, providing he has applied himself enough to make sergeant during all those years."

He stood up and stretched. "I can't say that I regret my decision, to lead black troops, that is. They are really no worse than whites, and many are much better. Attitude is very important in a soldier, and these men may feel this can give them a chance to prove themselves and their race. The Indians fear them, you know, and that fear is justified. We find them very courageous after they once taste battle. In some cases, that courage is unbelievable, almost foolhardy! I've had a few run, but then, who doesn't run when you find bullets around your ears?"

I sat back and thought about that for a spell. "Reckon I was lucky," I told him. "I'm only twenty-two and I was a bit young to serve durin' the war years. I had jest turned thirteen when it began, but I was doin' a man's work. Have been since I was nine. Soldierin' wouldn't be for me. Too many fellers tellin' you what to do. I couldn't put up with thet! I'm my own man!" I chuckled. "Sometimes thet has got me into a peck of trouble, come to think of it, but none I couldn't handle."

We talked for another half hour, then turned in. I had a hard time getting to sleep for a time. Nell was constantly on my mind. I thought of all the bad things that could happen while we were apart. Donelson's bearded face appeared with that gold tooth gleaming in the moonlight, and I felt a chill of fear crawling along my backbone. Surely he'll run for the border, I thought, now that the Army is so close behind him. He won't dare go back to the mountains! I tossed and turned fitfully before finally dropping off to sleep.

* * *

We rolled out early, about an hour before sunrise. I had slept in my buckskins, leaving my knee-length moccasin boots on my feet, so I headed directly for the privy. Afterwards, a quick wash from my canteen put me first in line for breakfast. The cook that morning was the same private who'd let me share his tobacco.

Altogether, it was the best meal I'd had for a spell. I poured a second cup of coffee and walked over by Waggonier. He was sipping at the rim of his cup and staring out across the desert. It was still a half hour to sunup and not all that easy to see in the false light of dawn. He appeared a mite worried, and I asked him why. After all, it was early, and his men would have a long ride on their return.

"I doubt your corporal got very far last night, 'less'n he could see in the dark. It's mighty rough goin' for horses, and he wouldn't want to lame his saddle stock. Why don't we leave right now with the men you have here. After all, he is just one man; Donelson, I mean. We won't need an army to ketch him or kill him, as the case may be." I wasn't sure but what I'd get Waggonier's dander up again, him having an awful short fuse, as I'd found out yesterday.

Surprisingly, he was smiling when he turned around. "It is obvious you'd never make a soldier," he told me. "You're totally lacking in responsibility. We can't go off wandering in the desert, hoping to run across Donelson. I have to do things the Army way, and that means we wait here until I have my entire command intact. I told the corporal to stop when it became too dark to see the trail. By now, he should have made contact with the others and be riding back before very long. I estimate they will be here about ten or so."

Sipping at his coffee, he squinted at me over the rim of the cup. "That doesn't mean you can't leave," he said. "We will be riding south, and your wagon is at Fort Bayard. Why don't I give you an order releasing the wagon, and you just go on your way. How does that sound, Bailey? No reason for you to hang around here when you have machinery to deliver. Then too, the sooner you can get back to your lady, the better your chances for reconciliation. Come along. Let's get out my field desk, and I'll write the order.'' He took me by the arm, and we walked toward his bedroll.

I had to make a hard decision. I wanted to recover my wagon and do the job I was being paid for at the same time that I wanted to be there when they caught up with Donelson. To me, he was more like a ghost than a real man. I'd had only that one glimpse of him while he was doing his best to beat me to death. Then I got to thinking about how much I wanted Nell and how I had to make a start somewhere along the line. If I was to try and get her back, I'd be in better shape by clearing the board, finishing the job I was hired to do. I made my decision! I'd go to Fort Bayard to get back my wagon, and to hell with Donelson.

Waggonier wrote out the order and gave me directions for reaching the fort. ''You should be there in four hours, barring something unforeseen.'' He gave me his hand. ''Wishing you good luck is a pleasure,'' he said. ''From all you've had to say, your lady is well worth the effort. Perhaps we will meet again, Bailey. Hopefully under happier circumstances.''

Didn't take long for me to saddle my horse and gather up the mule. I stepped up on the bay and lifted a hand to the rest of the men. ''Thanks, fellers. You take care now. I'd give you all an invite to the weddin', but I ain't sure jest when it'll be or where. Wish me luck! So long, now.''

The bay was restless and wanted to run, but I reined him back to a steady lope. I'd borrowed a small measure of corn from the troopers' supply, and I fed it to him before I turned in the night before. I'd let him eat it out of my palm and watched as he rolled it around in his mouth, grinding it between his big molars and swallowing it with relish. He'd been the best horse in my string when I'd worked that drive for the McCowan brothers. Young and full of vinegar but a top-notch cowhorse. He didn't care much for cattle and had a habit of snapping at their rumps when we drove them. Now and then he'd get more'n just skin, and that steer would be long gone! After a time, I reckon some of the regular bunch quitters got to know him, and they'd run for cover.

After we'd got to Abilene and sold the two herds, we had a choice of quitting right there or going back to Texas. I had elected to go back, and so had most of the others. Rush McCowan, who was the oldest brother, had let us pick out two horses for the return and told us they were ours to keep. Naturally, I'd taken the bay, along with a mouse-colored old gelding that had been my night horse. Rush taken the time and wrote out a bill of sale to each man so's there'd never be no arguments about ownership. Nice feller, that Rush. I wondered what he was doing right now.

Over to my right, the sun was just beginning to show. It was red and brassy, a sure sign of a hot day to come. Nell and Pop would be up by now and packing to travel. I would have to start backtrailing them from that camp; hopefully, the sign would still be clear enough to read when I finished delivering the machinery and collected my money.

Something caught my eye, and I looked up at two buzzards banking and turning in the air. I wondered if they weren't maybe the same two that had scared Braunt so badly. It was possible, I guessed. I watched as they soared up, up, till they seemed to hang there motionless for a moment, only to drop off on one wing and glide effortlessly without moving a feather, their heads down and their eyes searching.

The bay snorted and jumped aside as a rabbit broke from a bit of brush and ran out ahead of us. I whistled shrill as I could, and the rabbit stopped and peered around. Next moment he was gone again. I laughed, and the bay snorted to show his disgust but kept up his steady pace. Looking down at the ground, I could see wavy lines in the sand where one of them sidewinder rattlers had passed, probably hunting for some shade in a land where there was precious little.

I felt pretty good, I guessed. Sure! I had to figure my chances with Nell weren't all that good, but they'd tally to fifty-fifty, I reckoned. She loved me, I was sure of that. But I'd made her feel cheap without meaning to, and now she was running from me. It'd take some tall talking, but I had to convince her somehow that I loved her, too, and wanted us to spend the rest of our lives together. Surely she could be made to believe that. Well, I'd sure find out!

After a couple of hours I pulled up and got down. Time to walk for a spell. First I tied the bay to a bush so's I could sponge his mouth and nostrils out with a wet neckerchief. I did the same for the mule, then taken a swallow of water for myself. The sun was mighty hot, and the air was still as could be. Not a hint of a breeze. I bunched up that wet neckerchief and wiped my face and neck, then tied it around my head. I was sure wishing I'd taken back my hat. I'd see if I could buy one from the sutler at Fort Bayard.

We walked for about a half hour, and then I stepped back onto the horse and kicked him into a lope again. Far ahead, it seemed I could make out a clutter of buildings. Distance is deceiving in the desert, because the air is so durn clear.

Another half hour went by, and I could tell now that it was the fort I had seen. Still about five miles off, but I could see a flag, or something like one, waving atop a pole, and little dots that had to be men were moving around. It was more or less downhill from here, a gently sloping grade that made the going easy.

As we got closer in, I could see that Fort Bayard was not exactly a spit 'n' polish post. It had a series of long, low huts made out of a collection of logs and round stones, with flat, dirt roofs that more'n likely leaked during the infrequent rains. The windows were hinged to swing upward, and right now they had props holding them open. There were no walls, like you'd be expecting to see. After all, a fort is a place that's walled in for protection. This looked more like shantytown in Denver. I sure didn't envy the men who had to live there.

A sentry at the gate told me where I could find the quartermaster. Seems he was the one who kept such property in trust. I trotted the bay across the compound and toward a long building with a pole corral alongside. Off to my left a ways I could see what must be the sutler's store. Indian blankets, washtubs, and such were hanging on racks outside the building. At one end a wide awning sheltered a cluster of crude benches, and a dozen or more troopers were drinking from mugs and talking in a desultory fashion. One pointed, and all heads swung around toward me. The hum of conversation carried across the parade ground, and I sensed that the talk had to do with me, or at least a good part of it.

The quartermaster sergeant was a short man with a cheery face that somehow seemed out of place. He was fat and the blackest man I'd ever seen. He was middle-aged, and his whitened hair clung to his head like tufts of cotton. I gave him the order Waggonier had written, and he perused it, nodding as a particular line seemed to corroborate something he had expected to see. He read it through to the end, then pursed his lips in thought for a moment. "I reckon you'd best report in to the headquarters building," he told me. "Your wagon's here in the fort, and it's safe enough. You get the top sergeant to okay this, and I'll hand over the wagon." He pointed out the building with a wave of his hand.

"The one with the porch," he said. "Just tell the sentry at the door that you wanna see the top. If he gives you any back talk, you just point over here and tell him Sergeant Dugan told you to report in. Don't take no sass off of that young whippersnapper, you hear! Now, you run along, sonny, 'cause I got lots of work to do. When you come back, I'll get some help to harness your team, and you can be on your way. Give me them reins, and I'll put your horse and mule in the shade somewhere. Maybe give 'em a bit of grain."

I handed over the reins and watched him waddle away. He had found a home in the Army, that was plain to see. Dugan! The name fit him fine. He had all the assurance of an Irish politician and knew where he stood. He hadn't made a crack about my buckskin clothes, hadn't even seemed to notice them at all. I doubted that anything would bother him.

Right now I just wanted to get my wagon and drive it on out of the fort. The place gave me the creeps. Looked more like a prison camp than an Army post. I gave a hitch at my breech-cloth and started toward the headquarters. I had to pass the sutler's store along the way, and I didn't get far before trouble began. I should have known that it wouldn't be all that easy. Nothing ever was, leastways not for me!

"Hey, Injun!" One of the troopers had jumped up and was hollering at me. He gripped a mug drunkenly in one hand as he repeated the hail. "Hey, Injun! What're yew doin' heah? This ain't no damn agency! This yere's Fo't Bayard! They's no agency beef heah foh yew red niggahs! Yew bettah git on outta heah, and ah mean now, befoh ah cuts yew from yore red butt all thuh way to yore brisket. G'wan! Git movin'!"

Last thing I wanted was any more trouble. I ignored him and

kept walking. Looking back, I could see other troopers hauling
at his arms, forcing him to sit back down at the bench. All I
needed was a fight, and I'd never get my wagon out of that fort.
Be lucky if I didn't wind up in the post stockade. Then I'd never
see Nell, not ever again!

The sentry at the door wasn't all that ready to let me go in. He
was young, all right, maybe eighteen or so. Looked me up and
down and didn't seem to believe what was standing before him.
He brandished a Springfield across his chest and a belligerent
scowl on his brown face, and he ignored the paper I was holding. That is, until I mentioned Sergeant Dugan. The rifle came
down, and he reached over and opened the door.

"Yes, sir," he told me. "You go right on in. The top's at
that desk, right there." He stood aside as I entered.

The wooden placard read SGT. AMOS WELDERMAN. A taci-
turn, dour man, he listened silently as I explained how I'd lost
my wagon to the two deserters. His eyebrows lifted briefly as I
told about killing Braunt and burying his body under a pile of
rocks, but he didn't seem impressed. He let me tell the whole
story without saying a word. Then he reached into a drawer and
pulled out some paper, a bottle of ink, and a wooden penholder.
Searching in a corner of the drawer, he found a point that
seemed to please him and then fitted it into the holder. Apparently a methodical man, he carefully wrote down a few words,
making certain the pen would function.

"You just sit down there in that chair, Mister Bailey. Now
tell me exactly where you buried Braunt's body. Be sure you include any prominent landmarks that might help in locating the
grave. First, would you care for some coffee, sir? We have a
fresh pot right here."

When I said yes, he shoved back his chair and stood. He was
something to see, let me tell you! He hadn't appeared a tall
man, but he had to be at least six-eight. He was slender and
wiry and seemed to uncoil as he got out of the chair. His legs
were uncommonly long and noticeably bowed, and his arms
hung almost to the floor, or so it seemed. When he returned
with my coffee, I noticed the knuckles on his hands. Criss-
crossed with scars, they were knotted and oversized. He had

had a fight or two, I reckoned, and I doubted if he'd lost a single one. With that reach, nobody could get in close.

After I'd told most of the story and mentioned the rocky spire near the grave, he gave me the paper to sign. "You're free to leave, Mister Bailey, as soon as you're of a mind. The sutler has some civilian clothing if you want to change out of those buckskins. His prices aren't cheap, and the clothing is used, of course, but clean and in style. He buys from the recruits as they are enlisted, then turns around, making it available to men being discharged." A slight grin crossed his lean face. "A clever way of doing business, wouldn't you say? A clever man, the sutler. Indeed. A clever man."

I finished my coffee and thanked the sergeant. Told him I planned to hang on to my Indian outfit, but I did need some sort of hat. "I might be interested in some honest-to-gosh white man's pants, you know, with a seat that would cover up my behind. Then too, I could use a belt gun. Donelson took mine, and I reckon he still has it. I'm sure the Army can't sell me one, but mebbe you know somebody that's got an extra revolver they'd sell. I got some cash money, not a lot but enough to git by."

He nodded. "Here! Take this back and give it to Sergeant Dugan. It's the paper you brought from Lieutenant Waggonier. Guns are usually included in the sutler's stock. Used guns that he buys from men enlisting in the Army. Even if they choose not to sell immediately, he will eventually get all of their personal property. Guns, watches, rings; everything goes to August Grebs sooner or later. At first, it's not considered an outright sale. They 'borrow' on their possessions in order to get money for liquor and gambling. Grebs charges, of course, for the privilege. His interest rates are higher than most, and the men never seem to retrieve their gear. I have even seen Indians pawning their jewelry, some of it the finest silverwork you ever saw. They never get it back!"

I stared at him in amazement. "Why do you let him cheat them like thet? Can't you do somethin' about it? Don't he ever make nobody mad enough to jest *take* back their stuff?"

Welderman shook his head. "The Army has no jurisdiction. The sutler works under the Indian Department. Well, I'll be letting you leave now, Mister Bailey. Thank you for your help, and I wish you luck. Have a safe trip to Lordsburg.'' Holding out his hand, he told me to be careful in my dealings at the sutler's and thanked me again for telling him of Braunt and Donelson and giving him the location of Braunt's grave.

As I walked through the door, I figured I'd better try to buy myself a hat before I hitched up the wagon. The same batch of troopers was still under the awning, and that one loudmouthed drunk glared at me as I passed by.

Grebs turned out to be a man in his thirties, with a big handlebar mustache. Judging from his florid complection, he sampled his own whiskey frequently. He made a show out of greeting me and came out from behind the counter with a big smile. His voice was loud and his manner boisterous.

"You're Bailey, I guess. Well sir, I must admit that I am just a mite disappointed to see you.'' He laughed and grabbed my arm. "C'mon, let me buy you a drink! On the house! Maybe I'll just have one with you, although it's just a bit early in the day for me.''

Reaching under the counter, he brought out a dark bottle with a label showing a six-point buck. "This Royal Stag has to be the best rye whiskey in the territory,'' he said. "You probably never tasted a smoother drink.'' He poured out some of the murky fluid and handed me one of the glasses.

"Well, Bailey. Here's to women, whiskey, and wealth, and the good health to enjoy them all!'' He tipped up his glass and drank the contents in one swallow, smacking his lips in loud appreciation. "Man, that's good stuff!''

I had sipped at mine, and it wasn't all that bad. Better than most of the whiskey you'd find along the border. Tossing down the rest, I handed him the glass with my thanks.

"Mighty fine whiskey, Mister Grebs. Right now, I'm in sorta hot water, and I need to git my business done and be on the way to Lordsburg. I'd like to buy a hat, and mebbe you have a pair of pants thet'd fit me. I'd already spotted a case full of pistols and was headed that way.

"Don't be in such a hurry,'' he told me. "Here! Have another drink. You'll go a long ways before you find sipping whiskey like this. Besides, I have a little business I'd like to discuss with you, and it would be worth your time to listen. Might just solve your money problems, too." He sat me down at a table and went back for the bottle.

As soon as he'd turned around, I got out of the chair and went to the pistol case on the counter. There were two Colt Navy revolvers and one .44-caliber Army model, along with a pair of Remingtons and several other guns I couldn't recognize. Apparently, both Navies had belonged to the same man, because there was a belt with two holsters attached lying alongside them. The leather was nicely carved, and the belt buckle looked to be solid silver. The guns themselves had most all of the original finish, and the stocks were ivory.

I figured they were too rich for my blood, so I picked up the .44 Army and looked it over. It also had a holster and belt, with a small pouch for percussion caps held by a loop. The gun was worn but seemed to be in good order. Carefully easing back the hammer, I tested the action, and it was very tight and crisp. Punching out the barrel wedge, I took down the barrel, using the loading lever to start it. I squinted down the bore, and it was bright and clean. It was really a fine gun, one with lots of use but showing loving care. It was a heavier caliber than I was used to, but I decided I'd buy it if the price was right. Before I put it back in the case, I noticed two initials carved into the bottoms of the walnut stocks. Crudely done, probably with a jackknife, was a C on one side and an A on the other. They could have stood for "Confederate Army" but more likely were the initials of the gun's former owner.

Grebs had noticed me at the counter, so he put the bottle on the table and came over to join me. "See anything there that you can't live without?" he asked. "If you want a pair of really fine guns, take a look at those Navy Colts. I can give them to you at a ridiculously low price, by the way. I got 'em pretty cheap, and I'd pass that on to you."

I nodded and looked back at the guns. "How much are you talking about?" I asked. "Can't be too much, because I have only a few dollars here." I held out my hand with only one of my double eagles and some loose silver, about twenty-two dollars in all.

"To tell the truth," he told me, "I was planning to ask a bit more than you have there. But you never know. Maybe, just maybe, we can put together a deal and you'll walk out with those two pistols strapped around your middle."

"I don't understand," I said. "What do you mean? I need a belt gun, but I figgered thet .44 was more in my range. I ain't never owned one, but I've heard lots of fellers really swear by them Army Colts."

He smiled and motioned me to follow him back to where he had left the bottle. Pulling the cork, he poured each of us a generous drink. "Sit down," he told me. "Sit down, and I will put it to you straight. I *need* that wagon, and I mean I need it real bad! Before you came in here, I was sure the wagon was gonna be mine. Didn't think the owner would show because I was certain he was dead. The man who abandoned it out there was a fugitive, a deserter from the Army who was under sentence of death for killing another soldier. Stood to reason he had killed somebody else just to get the wagon. I'd already made arrangements through my Indian agent to buy the wagon from the Army. Give the money to the troop fund, which was put together to lend a hand to widows and orphans of troopers killed on duty."

He drank from his glass and leaned across the table. "I can pay you more than it's worth," he told me. "Cash on the barrelhead, right now! I'll even throw in those pistols as an extra boot. One hundred dollars and those guns. That's my offer. What do you say, Mister Bailey? Do we have a deal?"

I shook my head. "Nope. Sorry, Mister Grebs, but I don't intend to ever part with thet wagon. I need it too, and you ain't got enough money to buy it from me. Now, what'll you take for thet .44 Colt? I need a belt gun, and I need one I can count on. What's your price, Mister Grebs?"

He sat back in his chair like he couldn't believe what I was saying! Then he picked up my glass and poured the contents back into the bottle. Smacking the cork back with the flat of his hand, he scowled at me, his face red with anger!

"You ain't got enough money to buy one of my guns!" Rising to his feet, he looked down at me and sneered. "Twenty-*five* dollars for the .44 Colt. Too bad you ain't got it. I told you

I'd throw in the Navies as part of our deal, and I meant it. Now you can go looking somewhere else for a gun. You haven't got enough money to buy one from me." He started toward the bar, the bottle of whiskey in his hand.

"Wait up a minute," I said. "You said you got them guns pretty cheap. Jest how much was you plannin' to ask?"

He though that one out for a moment, and when he answered, it was clear he was just trying to play me for the fool. A crafty smile turned up the corners of his mouth, but I saw hatred in his eyes. "Forty dollars," he said. "That's all! Just forty dollars, and you ain't got but twenty-two. Ain't that too bad? Forty dollars would buy you a pair of pistols worth well over a hundred, and I'd throw in a pair of pants and a hat. That is," he added, "if you *had* forty dollars on you right now. Not an hour from now or even five minutes. You lay out forty dollars, and you'll buy yourself the guns, a pair of pants, and that hat you need so bad." He grinned.

A half dozen troopers had come into the store, attracted, I guess, by Grebs's loud talk. Looking over at them, I could tell what they thought of Grebs. They weren't exactly on my side, but they sure didn't care much for the sutler. He had lied and cheated and given them next to nothing, and this'd been going on for some time. Now they were waiting to see whether he would get his way again or maybe a well-earned comeuppance. I couldn't resist. Turning back to the scowling Grebs, I smiled and spoke my piece.

"In thet case," I told him, "I b'lieve I'll jest take 'em off your hands. Sound's like a bargain price to me, one I'd be a downright fool to pass up. You have yourself a sale."

While he stood there, his mouth hanging open, I picked up a pair of butternut jeans and held them against me to make sure they'd fit. A wide-brimmed felt hat caught my eye, one similar to Lieutenant Waggonier's. I tried it on for size and found that it fit perfectly, so I just left it on my head.

"Now," I said. "I b'lieve you said all this would cost a mere forty dollars. Is thet keerect? Fine, Mister Grebs! You jest made yourself a big sale. Thet oughta make your day."

I handed the astounded sutler two gold double eagles and

strapped on the double holster rig. Reaching down, I picked out
the two guns and slipped them into the holsters. Grebs just
stood there, his face twisted and turning purple. His breathing
increased until it threatened to strangle him. I stepped back a
pace when he started toward me. He had the bottle upraised as
if to strike, and there was murder on his mind.

"Now you jest hold it right there," I told him. "You're the
one thet put the price on these guns, and all I done was take you
up on it. Like I said, a man'd be a durn fool *not* to buy them! If
you want to fight, I'll fight you, but I've laid out my coin, and
this property is mine."

The troopers tittered, and one laughed out loud. Another
joined in, until they were all laughing. "He shore got yore
numbuh, Mistuh Grebs. Yessirree, Bob! This yere's one man
you cain't step on and not have him pay you some mind. The
joke's on you, Mistuh Grebs. This time the joke's on you!"

Grebs stopped and glared around the room. He could see
plainly that no one was about to sympathize with him. "You
tricked me," he muttered. "Told me that was all you had. A
twenty-dollar gold piece and two dollars in silver. You're a liar
and a cheat and you ain't gonna go out of here with those guns!
I'll have the provost marshal on you, and he'll leave you in the
stockade until you rot! You lied to me!"

I shook my head. "No, sir, Mister Grebs. You're wrong!
You got it all backwards. I didn't tell you no such thing. You
think back, now. What I really said was this, and I remember
real well. I told you I only had a few dollars *here in my hand*. I
didn't say thet was all the money I had. You're jest too quick to
jump the gun. I had another pair of these gold pieces stashed
away. No Mister Grebs. We got us a deal, and you ain't about
to back out of it. These men will gladly back me up if you want
to call out the provost marshal!"

I started to walk out but remembered something else I'd forgotten in all the confusion. "Oh, yeah. I'll need powder and
ball for these two Colts. Might even be a good idea to throw in a
bullet mold. Would you mind, Mister Grebs? I'd be much
obliged, you can bet on thet."

With a strangled oath, Grebs flung the whiskey bottle at my

head. I ducked, and it passed over harmlessly. Outside the door, somebody called out loudly. "Well! Thank you so much, Mistuh Grebs. We'uns is in yore debt, and we sure are thankful." One of the troopers had caught the bottle and pulled the cork, and he now was drinking the whiskey. Several more had him by the arm, trying to drag it down from his mouth. Most all were patting me on the back as I passed through. I had bested the crooked sutler and made a lot of new friends.

Halfway to the quartermaster stables, somebody cried out, and I felt the whiff of a bullet as it passed by my ear. A thunderous report followed on the heels of the bullet, and I spun around, my hand dropping automatically to the gun in my right-hand holster. I stood there staring with the useless Colt in my hand as Grebs cocked his pistol for another try. Suddenly, several men in the crowd of staring troopers staggered aside, and six foot plus of angry top sergeant knocked Grebs to the ground. Kicking the pistol out of his hand, he reached down with a long arm and jerked Grebs upright with a single powerful pull. Methodically, Welderman began hitting him across the face with the flat of his hand as Grebs dangled helplessly in his grip. Relentlessly, he continued slapping Grebs's face as it rolled from side to side, sodden blows that echoed across the compound. Grebs was barely aware of what was happening to him and made no effort to hit back. Finally, Welderman released his hold, and the hapless man dropped to the ground. As Grebs sat up, holding his arm across his face in fear, Welderman twitched his uniform into place and spoke to him menacingly.

"You aren't worth the sweat," he told him. "Now! You're through playing games with my men, you hear me? One more of your cute tricks, and I'm going to twist your ugly head off of that skinny neck. You get back in your store, and if you show your face outside, you're through in this fort! Forget your smart dealings and start doing the job you were hired to do. One step out of line, and that's it!" He turned toward the headquarters building and stalked off without a single word to me or any of the others.

CHAPTER 13

~~~~~~

SERGEANT DUGAN HAD A PAIR OF TROOPERS BRING out my team. The story of my dealings with Grebs was the talk of the post, it being the first time anyone had gotten the better of him. I had plenty of help in harnessing up, you can bet on that! A quick check of the wagon's load told me nothing was missing, and in no time at all I was ready to pull out. Stepping up over the wheel, I settled down in the seat and gathered the reins in my hands. At least a hundred troopers were gathered around the wagon, grinning at me and telling me how much they appreciated what I had done for them.

"Ain't nobody evuh got the best of thet man," one trooper told me, with a big smile on his face. Looking closer, I recognized him as the drunken soldier who had called out as I rode across the compound. He looked to be sober now.

Reaching out, he handed me a small packet done up in red cloth. "Heah," he said. "I b'lieve you was needful of this here. I ain't got no use fer it; not now. Them pistols you is wearin' was mine oncet upon a time. Thet devil Grebs is purty slick, but you done outtraded him and made him out a damn

108

fool. I thank yuh fer thet!'' He stepped back and was replaced by another, a big, strapping youngster who wore an even wider grin. He handed me a tail feather from a hawk.

"Here," he said. "I'd be obliged if'n you put this yere feather in yore hat. We been puttin' up with a lot from old Grebs, but we seen the last of thet. From now on, we'll git a fair shake, or Grebs'll be lookin' fer another store. You done give us the heart, and we thank yuh fer it."

As I whistled up the team and started the wheels moving, I looked over toward the corral. Sergeant Dugan and the tall, lean top sergeant were standing there together. I waved my hand in farewell, and they both lifted theirs in answer.

I waved again as we passed through the gate, and both of the sentries laughed and waved back. Lining the team for a distant hill, I got them started in the general direction of Lordsburg and then settled back in the seat. It had been a real interesting day and one well spent. Sergeant Dugan had taken a liking to me, it seemed, and had mentioned the possibility of me getting a freight contract hauling supplies from some point on the Ox Bow cutoff all the way into Fort Bayard. He said it would pay well, and the work would be steady.

That seemed like a heck of a deal to me, and I told him so. First I had to get rid of the mining machinery, and my next chore would be finding Nell and the old man. If I was lucky and they'd left some clear sign, I figured to be able to track them to their new campsite. I wondered how she was feeling, about now. Did she miss me or was she just tickled to death to see me gone? I'd find out sure as God made little green apples or betting that the sun would come up a ways to the east of me in the morning.

About an hour out, I stopped to rest the team and give a rest to my backside. I'd changed into the jeans before I'd left Fort Bayard, and they fitted real well. In the shade of some cotton-woods I rolled a smoke and unwrapped the red packet. Inside, I found a Navy-size powder flask, a nearly new brass bullet mold, and a hundred or so cast bullets. I figured the guns weren't much good without loads, so I took the time to charge them both. It felt real good, having the guns, I mean. The Winchester was a fine rifle but unhandy. With these pistols I was ready for most anything, like Bill Hickok would have been if he'd been in my moccasins. I laughed.

My face was clean-shaven except for several days' growth of beard. I reckoned that if I had been wearing a mustache, I'd maybe be mistaken for Hickok. He wore a buckskin shirt and carried two ivory-gripped Colts, just like me. I'd seen an issue of Beadle's *Pocket Library* not long back, and on its cover was a drawing of Wild Bill Hickok. They named him the Pistol Prince and pictured him rescuing a lady in distress.

That would sure be the life, I thought to myself. Having nothing to do but rescue ladies in distress and shoot a few out-laws from time to time. Hickok had life by the tail, on a down-hill pull. Of course, he hadn't just fallen into the life he led. I'd never seen the man, but I had heard he was hell on wheels with a short gun. Up in Santa Fe, word came through that he was running for sheriff of Ellis County, one of the toughest counties in Kansas. Hays City was included, and they ate a man a day in that town; or so I'd heard. The nickname "Wild Bill" had come after he'd wiped out the gang at Rock Creek Station up in Nebraska. A feller by the name of McCanless was the boss. Bill had shot him to death back in '61, along with part of his bunch. Until then, he'd been known as "Duck Bill" on account of the peculiar shape of an overly long nose. Or so I'd heard. I wouldn't want to say something like that in front of him, of course. A man could get himself killed real easy, and I had no real wish to die.

The mule had been pawing at the sand and uncovered a bit of water. Not much, just an oozing that was more mud than water. He sucked away at it until he'd satisfied his craving, then moved away and let the bay horse have his turn.

Glancing up at the sky, I decided I'd best be on the way. It wasn't more than three hours to sunset, and I had lots of miles to go. According to Sergeant Dugan, it was about eight or nine miles to Silver City and another forty more to go before I'd be in Lordsburg. I wasn't sure where that mine was located and would have to get directions in Lordsburg.

Tying the bay and the mule to the tailboard, I climbed up into

the seat and clucked to the team. Steadying them at a fast trot, I
settled back in the seat. Over to my right was Bear Mountain,
rising up a mile and a half into the sky. It meant an earlier sunset and less light to travel by. I decided to stop short of Silver
City and make my camp. Time enough to ride in early in the
morning and not run the risk of trouble with the local miners.
Sergeant Dugan had told me it was a problem for them. The
black troopers weren't all that welcome to begin with, and after
a few drinks the hoorawing would begin. It usually ended up
with somebody getting all shot up and sometimes killed. Better
to drive on in with plenty of light to see by and cooler heads to
deal with.

Another thing I hadn't considered until now: My load was a
valuable one, especially valuable to somebody who was needful of mining machinery and hadn't been able to find any. The
canvas fly covered it up but wouldn't keep a man from taking a
closer look. It wasn't so much that somebody would try to steal
it, but more that they might want to buy it from me and not be
willing to accept no for an answer. Right then I was wishing
that I had old Buck sitting on the seat beside me or, better still,
that this whole business was over and done with. Buck would
not only be company, he would scare off most anybody, big as
he was.

It was nearly sunset when I picked out a place to camp for the
night. Silver City was dead ahead, no more'n a mile or two, and
I could make out some tents and shanties almost like those back
in Fort Bayard. It was a shallow arroyo on the right side of the
trail, with a trickle of water running through. The banks
weren't too steep, and I had no problem guiding the wagon
down into it.

Once stopped, I wasted no time unhooking the team and pil-
ing the harness off to one side. I tied all four animals on fairly
short pickets so's they'd be in close and easier to keep in sight.
After that last experience, I wasn't taking any chances on being
jumped. I'd sleep real light, with one eye open, so to speak. I
really wasn't all that sleepy, having gotten a good rest the night
before, and I have to admit I was just a mite on edge.

The mess sergeant had given me a packet of food and some

coffee, so I went about getting my supper started. Firewood was abundant, nice dry mesquite that would burn hot without giving off much smoke. Willows grew along the banks and overhung the arroyo, so what little smoke did rise would be thinned out by the branches. I formed a small circle, using some rocks I picked up, and built a fire no bigger than your hat. Since I'd shot up my own coffeepot, I had to make do. A can of peaches was included in the packet, and they didn't last long, canned peaches being one of my favorites. I used the empty can to boil my coffee water.

Half a dozen slices of thick bacon, which I fried to well done, and a good-sized can of beans dumped in on top—that, together with a couple of hardtack biscuits, made up my evening meal. I'd intended to pick me up a bottle of liquor to take along, but the trouble with Grebs had made that next to impossible. It sure would have rounded out my supper.

I lay back against my saddle and thought about that. I wasn't really what you'd call a drinker. A sip or two now and then never hurt nobody. 'Course, when we hit one of them railhead towns, it might just be a different story. We tried our durndest to catch up on all the drinking we'd gone without, if you know what I mean. More'n once I'd woke up and hung onto a splitting head, swearing by all that's holy that I'd never drink another drop. Actually, it was a scary thing when you considered that we were packing six-shooters and could easily do something we might regret later on.

Getting out my pouch, I rolled a cigarette and lit it on an ember I picked out of the fire with two sticks. The sky was mighty dark, and not a single star was showing. I barely made out the moon, which was no more'n a patch of light on a thick black cloud. It could well rain before morning came, and I'd best consider that. Flash floods were not uncommon in this country. As a matter of fact, they were more the rule than the exception. But I was safe enough. I didn't plan to sleep all that soundly, and I figured there would be plenty of warning if high water did come.

A horned owl sounded his *whoooo, who, who,* and off in the brush I heard a rustling as some small critter hid himself from the night-prowling meat eater. A breeze had come up, a soughing wind that made the willow leaves flutter and moved puffs of sand from the banks of the arroyo. I could smell a dampness in the air that could mean the rain wasn't too far off and could fall on us very soon.

Figuring it was better to be safe than sorry, I decided my team should be in harness and hitched to the wagon in case the arroyo flooded. The team wouldn't be happy, but I would feel a heck of a lot safer. By then they'd have eaten a bit of grass, and I could add a quart of corn later.

Untying the picket ropes, I brought them over to the wagon and threw the harness on their backs. Within just a few minutes, I put the collars on, fastened the belly bands, put the bits in their mouths, and buckled both throat latches in place. Next came the yoke and breast straps, and lastly the breeching tugs, which I snapped onto the singletrees. Mollie gave me some trouble, of course, her being a mare. Reaching around, she tried to bite my arm and missed, but she managed to step on my foot. Old Jobe, he just stood there while I hooked everything up and never let on that he was upset.

From where the wagon was setting, I'd be able to climb up the bank with little trouble. Tying the team securely to a tree trunk, I went after the horse and mule. Wouldn't you know, the mule had managed to slip his rope and was off in a deep patch of brush, chomping away at the leaves. I could barely hear him and couldn't see a durn thing. Figuring he'd stay there for a while, I fetched the bay over to the wagon, tied him to the tailboard, and went back to scout out the mule.

By the time I caught up to him, it had begun to rain. In working his way into that brush, he'd managed to get tangled up in the branches. The picket rope was caught up in several of them, and it wasn't all that easy to free. Finally I worked him loose, and we started back to the wagon. I heard something but couldn't figure it out at first. A loud and heavy sound, it was coming closer by the minute. Mixing in was a rattling noise like pebbles rolling down a tin roof.

Suddenly, I knew. Water! A flood wave rushing down that

arroyo, carrying sticks and stones, and even big logs if it could find some. We had minutes or less to get to safety!

Grabbing the mule's halter, I began to run as fast as my legs would carry me, dragging the mule along. When he chose to balk, I jumped on his back and pounded my heels into his soft underbelly. He took off with a rush, and for a time I had trouble hanging on.

There was a lot more water running down the arroyo, and I wondered if we'd make it out of there in time. The mule was slipping and sliding in the wet sand and would have fallen if I hadn't jerked his head up in time. When we got back to the wagon, I jumped off his back and let him go on where he pleased. I'd look for him in the morning. Vaulting up into the wagon seat, I grabbed at the reins and tried to get the horses moving. When nothing happened, I cursed; jumping to the ground, I ran over and untied them from the tree. It just goes to show you; never lose your head in an emergency, no matter what! A little mistake like that could have cost me my life. Climbing back up, I hollered and whistled at the team to get going. Pulling back on the right-hand rein, I turned them up the bank with the back wheels slipping in the loose sand and the wagon box scraping bottom. For a moment I was sure we were goners. I could *see* it now—a monstrous wave thundering along the wash, carrying debris and big logs high on its crest. Black, frothing water that could crush anything in its path and leave us dead and mutilated.

The team dug in and heaved tight into the collars as my curses beat on their ears and my whip raised welts on their rumps. That wall of water hit the back of the wagon, and we slewed over sideways on the bank, with the tailboard buried and water flowing over the sides. The bay horse let out one loud scream and vanished. Frantically, I lashed out at the team, urging the horses to pull. "Pull! C'mon, you devils," I hollered. "Pull your hearts out! You can do it! Pull!"

Just as I was about to climb out over their backs, I felt the wagon move. Slowly, straining away, both horses leaning into the collars with all their might, we edged up the bank, moving ever so slowly onto drier ground and safety at last.

Jumping down, I grabbed them by the bridles and led them under a big cottonwood. Soothing and praising, I calmed them until they quit fighting me and settled down. I'd have to stay right there until daylight came. Raindrops as big as grapes were pelting me, driven almost parallel to the ground by the strong winds. There wasn't any way to escape the buffeting. I just pulled my hat down over my ears, tied it with my neckerchief, and leaned into Mollie's neck, holding on as tightly as I could. She shifted from one foot to the other and answered with a grunting whicker.

CHAPTER 14

~~~~~~

DAWN CAME RELUCTANTLY, WITH DARK, SULLEN clouds obscuring the sun. I found myself curled up next to Mollie, who stood head down with her tail tucked between her legs. Jobe and the mule, who had apparently gotten lonesome, were close beside her, taking advantage of each other's body heat. I was stiff and sore from standing there for gosh knows how many hours, and I had no recollection of ever lying down. I guessed that my concern over the animals had kept me from getting into the wagon, where I could have stayed warm and dry.

By turning over some deadfalls and searching under trees, I was able to come up with some dry wood, and I lost no time starting a fire. My clothing was soaked, and my buckskin shirt had stretched and lengthened from its own weight and now hung past my knees. Once my fire was going good, I stripped down to the buff and hung everything over the fire.

My roundup bed was under the wagon fly and had kept dry, so I wrapped myself in a blanket and set about feeding corn to the animals. A quart of corn was worth a day's graze as far as perking them up, and in no time at all they seemed to be feisty and ready to roll.

After I'd eaten some bacon and hardtack, washed down with about a quart of boiling-hot coffee, I felt some better. My clothes weren't really dry, but I was eager to move out. It could well start raining again at any moment, and I had lots of miles to cover. The water was still rushing through that arroyo, but it couldn't last much longer. As parched as the ground had been, it would be soaked up before long. Even at that point, the crossing was no more than hub deep. I had no doubts about braving it, but first I had to try to locate my bay horse. The poor devil hadn't had a chance when that huge wave had hit us, and he could have been miles from where we were. Still, I had to try. Saddled and bridled, he wouldn't stand a chance of surviving by himself.

First putting Mollie and Jobe out on long pickets, I rigged a war bridle for the mule and mounted up. He wasn't in complete agreement with my plans, and we wasted ten minutes or so deciding who was the boss. After buck-jumping, twisting and turning, and trying to roll me off, he finally realized I was there to stay and gave in. We set off at a hard racking trot, which appeared to be his one and only gait.

I found the bay horse almost immediately. Swept away by the monstrous wall of water, the luckless gelding had drowned and was held in a tangle of debris almost three-quarters of a mile down the arroyo. I managed to retrieve my saddle and bridle, both in a somewhat battered condition but still worth saving. Two buzzards sat on the limb of a gnarled and twisted pinyon, heads hunched on bare, skinny necks and eyes fixed unblinking on the carcass of the dead horse. Again I couldn't help but wonder. Nah! They couldn't be the ones I'd seen before circling over Braunt as he lay dying. But it *was* possible, I guessed. We weren't too far from where I had shot and killed him, and those birds covered a big chunk of the countryside. I hated to leave the horse unburied but couldn't do anything about it. He'd been one fine cowhorse, and I was going to miss him a lot.

Curious to see what lay beyond, I walked the mule up on a

slight rise overlooking the arroyo to the south and saw an old lobo wolf chewing away at a dead steer. He'd opened the belly and was in it headfirst, with only his rear end showing as he tore away the soft entrails in huge bites. Sensing we were there, he backed out and raised his snout. One short sweep and he'd found us. For a moment I was sure he would run, but he didn't. The lure of all that meat was too strong, and he just stood there, daring me to do anything to him and ready to fight if I did. He was big, but his ribs showed gauntly. Chances were, he hadn't had any luck finding live game, and this was just too darned good to pass up.

I didn't bother him none. This was apparently somebody's grazing land, and him being there would keep off the coyotes and wild dogs. A wolf kills only when he's hungry, but a coyote or a wild dog will pull down a calf just for the fun of it. Both are scared to death of wolves, who have strong, unrelenting territorial codes and will chase down and kill any animal who violates them. Wild dogs and coyotes ran together in these days and were known to interbreed, but even a pack backed down from the wolves. This old-timer was ready for most anything. "You go right ahead and eat all you want," I called out. "You sure as heck ain't botherin' me, and I won't fool with you." I turned the mule down the slope and headed for where I'd left the wagon.

Silver City was booming. The road through town was wide and had a collection of tents and put-together shacks lining both sides. Halfway down on one side, a two-story structure loomed up, the raw, unpainted planks darkened by the rain, a saloon and hotel by the looks of it. A newly painted sign lettered across its front read TIMMER HOUSE. Several buggies and buckboards stood out in front, and at least a dozen horses were tied at the rail. Freight wagons and high-sided ore wagons were parked haphazardly along the muddy street.

I was tempted, I had to admit that! A drink or two would have tasted mighty good about then. My clothes were still damp, and it was a wet and chilly day. Whiskey would've helped to warm my insides and maybe even cheered me up some.

About the time I'd made up my mind to keep moving on, the

door to the saloon opened, and a man staggered out. Pockets turned inside out and clothes in disarray, he wasn't able to stand, much less walk. Reaching out, he clutched at a stanchion that supported the awning and hung on for dear life.

As I watched, another man came out and said something to the drunk. Whatever it was, the drunk wasn't about to agree with him. He pushed the man away, pawing at him feebly with one hand. There were more words, and I saw the second man's hand drop to a holstered revolver at his side.

Jacking a round into the Winchester, I called out. "Jest you hold it right there," I hollered. "Back off and leave thet feller alone, or I'll drop you where you stand! I mean every word, mister, so you jest better take me serious. Now move away, and right now, or I'll drop you jest for the hell of it!" As I spoke, I wrapped the reins around the brake and stepped down to the ground. It wasn't none of my fight, but I ain't never been one to stand by and see a man killed for no reason. The drunk wasn't harming nobody, and fair is fair back where I come from.

The second feller was madder'n hell but didn't know what to do about it. I had him cold, and he knew that for sure. "Do you know who I am?" he blustered. "You're making a real big mistake, mister! I've killed men for less. This here's none of your business, and you got no right butting in. You put that rifle down and I'll let you go back to your wagon. I'm the marshal here in Silver City, and I'm arresting this man for stealing. He's going to jail."

I grinned and stuck the rifle's muzzle under his chin, a move that he hadn't expected, that was plain. "No, sir, I've no idea who you are, and as a matter of fact I couldn't care less. What I do know is easy to tell. You were gonna shoot this man, and for no good reason that I could see. I guess mebbe I *should* know better, but I don't, so you'd best shuck thet gunbelt and let it drop on the walk. Then back up and sit down there on thet bench."

His face a mask of hate and frustration, the man did as I had asked. Fumbling the buckle open, he dropped the gunbelt at his feet and backed up to the bench. "Go ahead," I told him. "Sit down and keep on sittin' there until I tell you different. Don't try no tricks or you're a dead man!''

Surprisingly, nobody interfered. There were at least two dozen men nearby, and not one lifted a hand to help the marshal. I figured it was too good to last, and at any minute somebody would stick in his oar, and I'd have to shoot him.

Bending down, I taken that marshal's revolver out of its holster. It was a nice gun but hadn't seen a lot of proper care. Lead and burnt powder were encrusted around the rear end of the barrel, and the cylinder turned sluggishly as if the base pin was fouled. The frame was lettered FREEMAN'S PAT. DECR. 9, 1862 HOARD'S ARMORY, WATERTOWN, N.Y.; it was a make that I'd never seen. Thumbing the hammer back to half cock, I turned the cylinder, plucked the caps off of each nipple, and threw the whole batch into the street. Placing the revolver back in its holster, I taken the drunk by his arm.

"C'mon, friend," I told him. "We'd best be gittin' outta here before this so-called marshal finds a helpin' hand. I think you can leggo thet post, now. Jest hold on to me.''

As we started toward the wagon, the angry marshal called out: "You ain't getting away with this, you know. Soon's I can get a posse together, I'm coming after you. No gunslick can come in here and flout the law like you just done. We ain't about to put up with it. That man's a thief!''

Turning, I put the drunk's arm over my shoulder and held him steady. "I don't see how this man coulda stole anythin' from you," I said. "His pockets is plumb empty, and he sure don't have nothin' in his hands. He don't even have no gun. Look's more like he's the one thet's been robbed, and I would bet you're the one who robbed him. Now, you jest sit tight on thet bench, and we'll be on our way. And don't be tryin' to foller us or I'll shoot your ears off! You hear me?''

Raising the drunk up into the wagon seat was like lifting a sack of wet feed, but I finally got it done. He lolled on back against the bow frame and fell into the box with both legs high in the air. I didn't have time to fool around, so I just left him there as I climbed in over the wheel. With the Winchester still pointing toward the marshal, I unwrapped the lines and whistled up the team. "Heeee yah! Let's git outta here!" We taken off with a rush, and in minutes I watched the last shack whiz by. I doubted if that marshal'd be able to raise a posse or if he'd even try. What I would do with the drunk, I had no idea, but I couldn't stand there and see him shot down in cold blood.

Five miles or so down the road, we came up on a pond full of muddy water. Pulling over, I reached back and shook the drunk awake. "C'mon, partner. Wake up! We gotta talk, and you ain't in any shape right now. C'mon, now. I ain't got all day. Wake up! Git on outta there!"

It wasn't easy, but I finally dragged him out of the wagon and laid him on the ground. He muttered and moaned but kept his eyes shut. Gathering up a few twigs, I got a small fire started and made some strong coffee. When he wouldn't drink it, I threw him in the pond, clothes and all. He came up sputtering and hollering that he was drowning, then discovered that the water was only a couple of feet deep.

"Why'd you wanna do that?" he asked me. "I've never done nothing to you. Leave me be! You just go on and drive out of here. I'll be just fine. I'm going back to sleep."

With that, he curled up, muddy clothes and all, and closed his eyes. I reached over and taken the whip out of its socket. Flipping it back over my shoulder, I swung it down and popped it right in front of his nose. "Now!" I bellered at him. "You git up on your feet, and you jest see how fast you can run down thet road! You hear me? Git up!" I popped it again, this time flicking him on the rump.

He let out a yowl and jumped to his feet, rubbing his behind vigorously. "You crazy or sump'n?" he asked. "Like I said, I don't wanna be helped by nobody. Ain't nobody cares what happens to me." He began to blubber, and tears ran out of his reddened eyes and left tracks down his dirty cheeks.

"Come on, mister," I said. "Jest drink some of this coffee. You'll feel better in no time. I can't jest leave you out here in the desert. You'll die. Don't you know thet?"

He finally accepted the coffee and drank it. Cautiously at first, but once he'd gotten it down, he asked for another cup. After the fourth, he was beginning to look around and ask questions. I told him what had happened back in Silver City and how that marshal had tried his best to kill him.

"Why would he want to do a thing like thet?" I asked. "I couldn't see where you was hurtin' him none. You sure 'nough didn't rob nobody. You ain't got penny one in your pockets. How much do you remember? Jest what was his reason? Oh, by the way, my name's Bailey, Jake Bailey. What's yours?"

Now, asking a man's name without he's willing to give it to you voluntarily ain't the regular practice out there. I just figured to cut corners and get down to the root of his trouble, but I had to start somewhere. In looking him over, I had seen that his clothes were of good quality and that he was not just another drunk looking for a handout.

He appeared to be about thirty years old and had kept in fairly good shape until now. Whatever had set him to doing this, this attempt to kill himself with liquor, must have been real important, and I had to find out what it was if I was going to be of any help. He stared at me like he was trying hard to make up his mind, and then he finally spoke his piece.

"My name's Elon Westermarck," he told me. "I'm a student of geology, and I've been prospecting in these hills for almost two years. About six months ago, I found what we all dream about: a placer that led back to one of the most valuable formations of gold, silver, and copper that anyone could imagine. A real mother lode! Naturally, I brought in some samples and had them assayed, even though I could do a better job myself. I thought it best to follow the accepted practice so that no one could dispute my claim.

"After I'd filed on it, I bought more tools and plenty of food, since I planned to stay out there until I put together a real stake, enough to hire a crew and really develop the property. I succeeded beyond my wildest imaginings! Hit a solid face of almost pure gold. Not very deep, just enough so that I wound up with over one hundred thousand dollars in cash. Beyond that face, the vein ran in a dozen directions, and with subsequent exploration I determined that I had the potential makings of the richest mine in the territory.

"Foolishly, I allowed myself to trust that man back there in

Silver City. He seemed to be an honest man, and I had to share my good fortune with someone. Not the gold itself, of course, just the good news. We began drinking, and I bought a few rounds for the house. Someone suggested we play a bit of poker, and I was quick to agree. After all, I'd been out there by myself for so long, and I was hungry for friendship and approbation. After a while, I guess the liquor was just too much for me, and I passed out. I woke up and found I'd lost every cent of my money. My so-called friend was there, and he told me I'd lost the claim to him as well, that I'd bet it all in an attempt to win back what I'd lost.

"What he wanted and what he intended to have was my certificate of ownership, and he threatened to shoot me if the paper wasn't signed and turned over to him. He wasn't able to find it on me and started searching the room. I guess I ran out and made it as far as the door, and that's when the scoundrel caught up with me. I was too drunk to resist him, but I honestly didn't remember where I'd hidden the certificate. I don't remember even now! All I do know is that my months of hard work were all for nothing, and I don't care! Not anymore! I'd just as soon be dead. I haven't a nickel left for supplies, and without them I can't work my mine."

"Here," I told him. "Have another cup of this coffee. I ain't sure how I can help you, but I'm sure gonna try. When a feller works his butt off to make somethin' of hisself and has it all taken away, he feels like it's jest about the end of the world! I know! I've had it happen to me, and if I'd not had the luck of the Irish and the help of a fine woman, I'd never have gotten it back. Not thet I had anythin' near to what you've lost," I hastened to tell him. "My money was all tied up in this here wagon and my livestock. Still, it meant the world and all to me, and I worked darned hard for it. Tell me, jest how much money would it take to buy them supplies you need? I ain't got much, but I could mebbe give you enough to start. I got more money comin' when I deliver the load on my wagon."

He got all excited, and we spent the next hour going over his plans. I still had twenty-six dollars, and he said that would give him enough to last for a month. "I covered up my shaft," he told me. "Hid all of my tools inside except for a pick and shovel. Those I cached in the brush nearby. I'd want you to be a full partner, Mister Bailey. After all, without your grubstake I wouldn't have anything. No! I insist on that. What's fair is fair, and I won't have it any other way. You join me as soon as you can, and we'll share every ounce. Here! We'll shake hands on that." He stuck out his hand and grabbed mine, a big grin on his grubby face.

"Look," I told him. "Why don't you jest consider this as a loan? You can pay me back out of your first big sale. It ain't fair for me to take a half interest in your mine. You worked too hard for what you found jest to give away a half interest for no more'n twenty-six dollars."

He shook his head. "It isn't just the money, Jake. When I get ready to sell my first shipment of ore, I'll need you. I'm not a brave man, and I admit it. What's to prevent some other man or men from stealing it, just like the marshal in Silver City? I'd be only one lone man and wouldn't have a Chinaman's chance. Also, I don't plan to let you just stand around while I do all the work. Believe me, you'll have to earn your share! You'll get in there and grub away at that facing, just as I will do. There'll be times when you will wish you'd never seen that mine. You'll be tired and dirty and sometimes discouraged, just like me. This won't be just a ride on a merry-go-round, you can count on that. You must believe me, Jake. It is a fair deal!"

Reluctantly I agreed, but I didn't feel all that good about it. Then I got to thinking about Nell and all that we could do with the money. Buy us a real big spread and have no worries about stocking it. What the heck! Elon knew I'd go along, and he was right. I told him to count me in.

"Too bad we can't drink on it," he told me. "But it's no doubt just as well we don't have a bottle. I'll never trust myself around liquor again. I swear to that!" He frowned. "Wait a minute," he said. "Wait just a gosh darned minute." He sat down and started unlacing one of his boots. Once he had the laces untied, he jerked off the boot and reached inside a concealed pocket. The lining had been slit open next to the seam, creating a fine hiding place. Triumphantly, he held up a folded piece of paper, dirty and frayed along the edges. He laughed and waved the paper in the air.

"I got it," he cried. "It's my certificate, my claim to the mine! It's been in my boot all this time. Thank God I had the sense to hide it. If I hadn't, I'd be dead, and the marshal would be rolling in wealth. We're rich, Jake! This means we'll have no trouble proving it's ours."

We had another cup of coffee, and I gave Elon my money, a pretty cheap price for half a gold mine. We rigged the saddle on the mule, and I gave him enough food to last for four days. That's how long he figured it would take him to ride as far as Fort Bayard, buy the supplies he needed, and move on to the mine. He drew me a map showing the route to the claim, and I agreed to join him as soon as I could.

"First off, I have to find the woman I told you about, along with the old man and the dog. It may take me a while, but you can bet we'll be there as soon as we can. You ride wide around Silver City and keep your eyes out for the marshal. I didn't figger he'd foller us, but for thet much he jest might. When you git to the fort, look up a Sergeant Dugan. He'll help you deal with the sutler there. I had a mite of trouble with the feller, but I got it straightened out. You keep to the brush and don't ride no ridges, and you'll make it jest fine. Here! You best take this here Winchester. I got these two pistols, and I can always buy another rifle."

We shook hands again, and his face was a study. "I just can't thank you enough, Jake. I'm unable to find the proper words, I guess. You won't regret this, I promise you that!"

I watched him ride away. His shoulders were squared, and his chin was high. He looked back once and waved. I waved also, then climbed up into the wagon. "C'mon, Mollie! Git goin', Jobe! We still got some miles to cover! *Heeeee yah!* Git goin', there! *Thweeee eee!* G'up, you beauties!"

CHAPTER 15

~~~~~~

We PULLED INTO LORDSBURG EARLY THE NEXT morning. I'd had about four hours of sleep the night before and let the team graze on a patch of good grass next to a creek. Turned out the company who'd ordered the machinery had an office in the town, and the man in charge accepted the freight right there on his dock. He rounded up some fellers to unload the machinery and paid me off in gold coin, for which I was thankful. Federal currency wasn't too well thought of yet, and some folks'd turn up their noses at it or discount it by half.

"We'd just about given you up for lost, Mister Bailey. When our representative in Santa Fe telegraphed us, he said you'd be arriving on the sixteenth. Here it is the fourth of September, and you're nineteen days late. What happened? Some Indian trouble? We've heard rumors that Victorio is on the move with his bloodthirsty Mimbreños. No one is safe with that devil on the loose! He's the worst killer of the lot."

He'd brought out a bottle of brandy and poured us each a generous shot. While we sipped at the fiery liquor, I spoke of my brush with the two fugitives. I said nothing about my rescue by Nell and the old man, nor did I mention them.

"Them two were one heck of a lot worse'n any Injuns. The one is dead now, and I killed him, but Donelson, the really ornery one, is still very much alive, and he's around here in these mountains. Until he's been caught or killed, nobody's safe. He'd kill you for the boots on your feet if he needed a pair. You keep an eye out for him. He's a big feller with a black beard and a lone gold tooth, right there." I pointed to my lower jaw. "You'll know him when you see him up close. Don't take no chances with him. He's a killer!"

Rising to my feet, I emptied my glass and offered a hand. "I gotta git goin' now. I thank you for everythin', and we might jest do business again one of these days. I could do what everybody else is doin' and take up mining. It seems there ain't much else in the way of work around here."

Before I left Lordsburg, I had a few things to buy. Just around the block from the mining office, I found about all I had needed in THE LORDSBURG MERCANTILE—J.S. Mitchell Prop. Mitchell was a jovial man, and doubly so when he found I had cash money to spend. I bought a wagon load of supplies, including all the food we'd need for six months and some extra clothing.

"Don't s'pose you got a nice old caplock rifle," I asked. "I mean a real fancy one. It don't have to be brand new or nothin' like thet, but I'd want it to be in good shape. One with a lot of carvin' and mebbe some silverwork."

Mitchell smiled and nodded his head. "Why, yes. I just happen to have what you're looking for. An old fellow needed a grubstake, and he traded in a fine rifle. Hardly shows any use at all, and it is about the fanciest one that I've ever seen. Wait right there; I'll bring it out." He disappeared behind some curtains.

A few moments later he returned and handed me a beautiful percussion rifle. Full-stocked of curly maple, it had a long octagon barrel and German silver hardware. Coin silver inlays were set into the wood: crescents, stars, hearts, and fish, all fully engraved. It was in beautiful shape, and the maker's name was on the barrel: R. BEAUVAIS—ST. LOUIS.

"That there's a chief's gun," Mitchell told me. "It came out of Saint Louie in '59, but the chief it was intended for had already died. That old-timer I got it from used to be a trapper, and he meant this as a gift so's he could trap out the tribe's hunting grounds. Never panned out for him, so I wound up with the gun. It is a beauty, isn't it? I'll make you a deal you can't turn down, Mister Bailey. Twenty dollars in cash money. How about that? Sound good?"

I nodded. "Yeah," I told him. "I'll take it. There's just one more thing I need, and that's a keg of rum. You got anythin' like thet? Don't have to be a big one, jest so's I can git it in a wooden keg and not a bottle."

Mitchell shook his head but brightened up after he'd had a moment to think about it. "I got brandy in kegs," he told me, "but no rum. Ain't got no rum at all. Nobody here has rum. Ain't like the old days, when the mountain men came around. That's all they'd drink! Demerara rum from the deep jungles of Guiana, dark as mahogany and powerful strong to a normal taste. Rum from Barbados when they could hide it away from the British Navy. Brought here by ox train, led by dirty, hairy men who traded it for beaver plews. Them were the days, my boy! A wonderful time for the traders." Voice husky and faltering, he looked right through me like I wasn't even there. It only lasted a moment, and then he was back to the present and all business again.

I settled for the brandy and paid him off in gold. He'd given me a horn of powder, some bullets, and a mold that'd been made for the rifle, so I loaded it before I started out. After all, ain't no sense in having a rifle if a body can't shoot it. I'd given up my Winchester and just had my Colts. Nothing that would carry for any distance.

About a mile out of Lordsburg, I stopped and fed the team some corn. Made a small fire and boiled coffee for myself. I had to make a decision, and it couldn't wait. Them tracks left by Nell and the old man would have been washed out by the rain. I'd have to more or less make a guess as to what trail they'd taken and try to pick it up.

Sergeant Dugan had given me an army map that showed most of the country within about a hundred-mile radius. It was one they called a topographic map, and you could make out all of the mountains and the hills and streams. Figuring I'd best use common sense and decide where *I* would have headed if I were on the run, I looked the map over for sheltered valleys and canyons that had plenty of water. There weren't many.

One that really caught my eye was about thirty-two miles or so due north of Silver City. It showed some cliff house ruins just south of where the west fork and the middle fork of the Gila came together. It looked to be a desolate area but one where there'd always be some water. If I had wanted to find a real hideaway, I would have picked that spot. The ruins might offer some shelter in a storm, and corn could be still growing there. I'd seen them before, fields tended by the Early Ones a thousand years ago. The ears were usually small, but the kernels were still fit to eat. Ground into a coarse flour, they could be used to make tortillas or shovel cakes. A man could survive on that if he had some meat from time to time, and wild goats ran those mountains.

Didn't take me long to decide. I had to start somewhere, and that looked to be a likely place. Even if they were not there, they could be somewheres close and find me. I whistled up the team, and we taken out of there on the run, Jobe trying hard to keep pace with the high-stepping Mollie.

That night, we stopped a few miles short of Silver City's lights. We'd made good time, averaging five miles per hour, but it had been a long day. I was really tired, and so were the horses. I stripped off all of the harness, then watched them roll in the sandy soil, legs flailing the air as their necks arched and they squealed in absolute delight. Afterwards I fed them each a quart of corn and drove the picket pins in under some willows where the coarse grass was abundant. Once the animals were taken care of, I set about fixing my own supper and laying out my roundup bed.

I built the fire next to a bank from which the light couldn't be

seen in the town. I had no desire to fight off that city marshal or
any of his friends. The creek held enough water for me to
bathe, and I couldn't wait to get in. Soon as the coffeepot was
on and bacon was frying in the skillet, them dirty clothes of
mine came off, and I lay down in the creek water. It was only a
couple of feet deep, but it was fresh and clean after the hard
rain. Felt real fine, and I rolled around and splashed water at the
horses. I'd bought bar soap in Lordsburg, not the sweet-
smelling kind but rather a long yellow bar with lots of lye content.

Once I'd gotten myself reasonably clean, I scrubbed my
pants and underdrawers and hung them in the wagon to dry. I
left off my hunting shirt when I dressed, preferring to wear the
new pants and shirt I'd purchased in Lordsburg. Perhaps in the
morning it would be cooler, and I'd need the buckskin to keep
warm. I'd bought plenty of woolen socks, and they sure felt
great on my callused feet. My hair combed, and dressed in my
clean clothes, I felt like a new man. A feller seldom gets a
chance to wash all over out on the trail, and you've got to take
advantage of it when you can. I strapped on my holstered Colts
and poured myself a cup of coffee. The new pot I'd gotten at the
mercantile would take a while to break in. Right now, the coffee tasted somewhat of its newness.

Sitting back from the fire, I sipped at the aromatic brew in silence. My thoughts were of Nell and of the short time we'd had
together. I sure did miss her and looked forward to finding her
soon. I wondered what she'd say. Would that dumb remark of
mine still be riling her, or would she understand and forgive
me? Surely she'd know I hadn't meant it the way it had
sounded. The Apaches were virtuous people, a claim that few
whites could make. I'd had a long talk once with a man who
had escaped from the Mescaleros after a year of captivity. He
had been only eleven at the time but still remembered the cus-
toms of the band and the way he'd been treated.

For instance, most whites thought of the Indians as being
dirty people. According to this feller, he had to bathe all the
time. Every day if there was water enough! They loved their
children, he told me, and would never punish or speak harshly to

them. Instead, the children might be told to run as fast as they could to the top of a hill without taking a breath or even opening their mouths, or perhaps sent to a far canyon to fetch back a bowl of water. That bowl had to be full to the brim when they returned. Another common way used to breed strength and endurance into a boy was to have him run several miles with his mouth full of water. When he returned, he spat out the water in front of the elders as a proof of his ability to withstand the temptations of thirst.

Seldom did an Apache warrior molest captive women until he had reached his *ranchería*. Even then it wasn't considered a manly thing to do. I shook my head. We sure do think a lot of ourselves and not much of others. 'Specially Indian folks. I didn't consider myself no angel. I'd done just about everything, and a lot of it bad, but I'd never deliberately hurt anyone for the pure fun of it. Many whites would shoot an Indian just to see him fall. I'd heard tell of an Indian being shot at from a trainload of folks, with some of them making bets as to whether he'd drop on the left side of his pony or the right. That was pure-D cruelty!

I wondered how long it'd be before Nell had her baby. I would try to be as good a father as I could. It was a new and scary experience for me, one I hadn't given much thought to, but I'd try to spare my young'uns from a misery like I'd had as a boy. Not that I'd coddle and spoil them. They'd have to do their share, but no more. The thought of being a father was a pleasant one. I'd teach my youngsters to ride early on, put them on a horse before they could toddle.

The coffee was boiling over, and I ran to take it off the fire. The bacon was done to a crisp but still edible. I'd have to do my daydreaming later. Right then I figured I had better eat and try to get some sleep. We had more'n thirty miles to cover tomorrow, and most of it hard going.

We were on our way before sunup next day. I made a wide detour around Silver City, keeping down in the canyons most of the way. I saw a rider or two, but far off, where they'd never bother me. It looked to be a nice day. Not a single black cloud in the sky, just a few puffy white ones. Birds were out, and it smelled clean and fresh after the rain.

After about three hours, I was tired of sitting, so I got out and walked alongside my wagon. I was on the lookout for a deer or an antelope and had the caplock rifle propped in a corner of the wagon seat. Fresh meat would be mighty tasty, and I wanted some. There was no telling how long before I'd find Nell and the old man, and I didn't want to use any of the supplies I'd bought unless I had to. We'd need them at the mine, and it might be months before we bought more.

I'd been walking for about a half an hour, when I spied a patch of green up ahead. Green meant water and maybe even an animal there for water. I decided to leave my wagon and go ahead on foot. It wasn't far, and I could come back before the horses even missed me.

With the rifle held across my chest, I moved forward real slow, and as I got closer, I was careful not to step on dry brittle sticks or scuff through the sand. Closer up, I saw that it was a dammed-up pond with willows lining the banks. Crouching down, I crept up to within twenty yards before it dawned on me that I wasn't alone.

Just ahead was a big buck and three doe deer. His head was up, and he was watching something on the far side of the pond. Whatever it was, I couldn't make it out. One doe was almost as big as the buck and appeared to be barren. I had only moments to choose, and I decided on the big doe. Holding a fine sight on a spot just back of her left shoulder, I touched off the rifle and ran forward through the smoke.

She was down and thrashing in the water. The others had taken off and were already out of sight. Watchful of those razor-sharp feet, I grabbed her by the nose, pinched down on her nostrils, and pulled her head back. One clean pass with my knife opened her throat so's she could bleed out, and it was done. I dragged her out on the bank and quickly field-dressed the carcass, propping the cavity open with a pair of sticks so the air could get to it. She was really fat and would dress out well over a hundred fifty pounds. I hung her in the crotch of a willow and went back to fetch the wagon.

When I returned, the carcass was down on the ground, with the hide peeled back and both loins missing. Scuffed bootprints were all around, and off to one side was a fresh pile of horse droppings. Cursing, I leaped down from the seat to take a closer look. Whoever had done it had naturally been in an awful hurry, and he had botched up the hide badly. Mad as hell, I slipped both Colts from the holsters and ran around to the far side of the pond. The horse sign led off toward the north, with the sprayed-out sand and length of the track showing that the horse had been running.

Who would want to do a thing like that? If it had been a hungry man, I would have gladly shared the meat. I doubted the thief had been an Indian. Indians would not only have taken the whole deer, they would have likely lain in wait and had their fun with me. Not just any Indians, but mean ones who would steal from anyone, even their own people.

Could it have been Donelson? I wondered. Surely he would be well on his way to Old Mexico by now. He wouldn't stick his neck out by hanging around here. Not with them soldiers out looking for him. He'd be a darned fool. No! It had to be somebody down on their luck. Maybe a miner, or even more likely a prospector who had no grubstake.

I stripped off what was left of the hide and wrapped the cuts of meat in a tarp. It would keep until tonight, when I could take more time and cut it up properly. The heart and liver lay in the water where I'd left them. Tiny fish tugged at the strips of meat, and a good-sized crawdad scuttled out of sight as I stooped to pick them up.

Putting together a small fire, I stuck chunks of liver on sticks and suspended them over the flames. I'd have me one fine lunch before moving on. While it cooked, I got out my horn and loaded up the rifle. Mitchell had sold me a piece of linen ticking, and it worked fine for patching. First I laid a bullet in my palm and poured powder over it until a mound covered the bullet. This, by rule of thumb, should be a proper charge. Picking out the bullet, I poured the black powder down the bore and set it by thumping the butt of the rifle on the ground. I'd cut the ticking into strips about one inch in width and rolled it into a ball. With the ball in one hand, I fitted the end over the bore and started one of the cast bullets in, ticking and all. Cutting the excess linen away from the ball, I rammed the charge home with one smooth stroke of the wiping stick. Withdrawing the stick, I slid it into the thimbled channel, and the gun was all ready to fire except for placing the cap. This I did, careful to leave the hammer at the half, or safety, cock.

The liver was not quite ready, so I got out my map, and a quick look told me this must be a portion of Bear Creek only sixteen miles north of Silver City. From there, I had to go almost due east, through Reading Canyon, to where the trails led north toward the cliff house ruins. If I'd been on horseback, I could have cut off some miles, but with the wagon I was forced to stick to the canyons. My distance estimate of thirty miles was a mite off. Looked like it would be just a little farther, about forty-five miles in all. Didn't make me no nevermind. I'd still get there before dark.

After I'd eaten most of the liver, I threw the rest to my finny friends and rolled a smoke. A cup of coffee would've tasted good, but I couldn't spare the time.

After letting the horses drink sparingly, I got the wagon rolling again, headed toward Reading Canyon. As we passed through, I could see Tadpole Ridge looming to the south, with a pair of red-tailed hawks wheeling in wide circles overhead, and I thought about them. Redtails mated for all of their lives, and if one died or was killed, the other would mourn until dead. Got me to thinking about Nell again and what a great time we would have together, partners for life! Not just a wife and mother of our children but someone who would work alongside me, sharing the good and the bad and a ripe old age, God willing.

Up ahead I could see the end of the canyon, and I reached into my shirt and drew out the map. According to what I could see, Sapito Creek should be only three more miles, and then I could stop and rest the horses. We'd driven twenty-eight miles, more than half the distance to the ruins, and averaged about the same five miles an hour. Both Mollie and Jobe were big horses. Not your little scrubs, but draft animals, that were used to pulling a big load. With no more'n we had in the wagon, they

probably could have gone all day without any real rest. Still, it
was better to take our time, and a little snooze would suit me
just fine.

Sure enough, little more than a half hour later I could see the
creek up ahead. Like Bear Creek, the bank was lined with willows and a couple of big cottonwoods. Pulling under one of the
large trees, I climbed down and knelt to take a drink and splash
some water on my face and hands. When I raised up to wipe my
face, something slammed into my head; a sharp report echoed
against the canyon wall, and a terrible burning pain lanced
through my brain!

Blindly, I staggered forward and fell into the water. A pierc-
ing whistle came from one of the horses as I scrambled madly
for cover. Another shot, and a bullet thunked into an old deadfall, throwing powdery splinters into my face. If I couldn't get
out of sight, and soon, I'd be a dead man.

Wiping the blood out of my eyes with my neckerchief so's I
could see, I drew one of the Colts and crouched down next to
the deadfall. Another shot clipped the tree trunk, and I saw a
puff of dirty white smoke rising up from a brush clump a hundred yards away. Thumbing back the hammer, rapidly, in
quick succession, I fired four shots into the clump and saw another puff of white smoke rise up as a bullet clipped me, this
time on the left shoulder. I was getting nowhere fast and had to
find better cover if I planned to go on living.

Just west of where I was lying, I could see what appeared to
be a cleft in the canyon face. Several big boulders lay in front,
and others were scattered nearby. It offered much more in the
way of concealment, so I decided to make a try for it. Thrusting
my right-hand gun into the holster, I got out the other and
pumped another three shots into the brush clump as I backed toward the cleft. Two more shots, and I had shot the gun dry, so I
turned and ran. Ran like I never ran before, heart pounding and
my head feeling like the top was coming off! I made it just as
another bullet burned my leg. Only a graze that barely drew any
blood.

Out of breath and hurting, I reloaded both Colts, watching all
the while, in case the drygulcher showed himself. A half hour

went by, and there was not a sign of movement from the brush clump. Just as I decided he'd given up and left, I heard a sound from up above me. Gravel and small stones rattled on the sides of the cleft and rolled down to the canyon floor. More stones followed, this time larger ones that bounded on past my head and came to rest in front of me.

Soon the pile was so high that I could barely see over it. Then I heard a voice, and in the dim recesses of my mind it sounded familiar somehow. I'd heard that voice before!

"Never thought you'd make it, mister," the voice gloated. "But as it pans out, you've done me a good turn. Drove the wagon back in here after I had to leave it for them soldier boys from Fort Bayard. They damn near got me. If I hadn't been half awake, I'd be in their stockade right now!"

Donelson! It was Donelson. Once more he had me cold! I shook all over, I was so darn mad. Then I was scared. All he had to do was cover me up with them stones, and nobody on this earth would ever know what had happened. I'd be buried in there, with no way to get myself out. He could just take the wagon and drive off. Nobody would know the difference. He called out again, jeering at me as he rolled another stone.

"You still alive in there? I know I hit you at least one time, maybe more. I seen you fall and saw the blood on the side of your head. How bad are you hurt?" He giggled.

"Not that I'm plannin' to help out. Nope! I got lots of places to go and things to do with that wagon. Sorry, cowboy. Ain't nuthin' personal. You jist happened to be in my way." I heard more noise from above, and another of the big boulders tumbled down, coming to rest above me. Desperately, I tried to squeeze farther back in that narrow cleft, but it wasn't possible. That was as far back as I could move.

Silence, now. Dust from the rocks had filtered into my eyes, and I wiped them furiously with my bloody scarf. It was unbearably hot, and my head ached something awful, but I tried to take my mind off it and figure out how to free myself from the trap. Far as I could see, there was no way to get out. I'd never be able to move any of those boulders in time. I'd just die from thirst and hunger, and it might not take all that long. I couldn't even sit down, and my wounds were giving me fits, aching and burning from my sweat. The sound of a rifle booming brought me to the rock barricade; a four-inch crevice allowed me to look out.

Donelson was up on the wagon seat. He had just set my rifle down and was aiming a pistol. Off in the distance, I could see a skinny, long-necked horse running flat out, dodging as Donelson fired the pistol. On his back was the old Indian who'd been called a coward. Right now he was lying alongside the horse, clutching at the mane with one hand as the black-bearded murderer tried to shoot him off his mount. Each time Donelson fired, Pop would swerve, but he kept coming, staying back just far enough so he wouldn't make too easy a target. He was whooping and hollering at Donelson and daring him to come and fight, or so it seemed. Spinning around on that old worn-out horse that I'd thought was about ready for the glue factory. It was really something to see! Then I heard another rifle crack, and Donelson ducked. Jumped on down to the ground and got under the wagon. Two more shots were fired, and dust was kicked up near one wheel. Another, and I could hear the outlaw cursing as he reloaded his gun.

I tried to bring my pistol into play, but the crevice was too high up. I had to stand on my toes in order to see any action at all. It was maddening just to stand there without being able to lend a hand to my own rescue. Nell had to be the unknown rifleman, but I couldn't spot her. No matter how I craned my head around and tried to get a glimpse, the cliff above me was hidden from my view. I hollered, warning her to be careful and not risk being hit.

"Keep him down, Nell, but don't show yourself. He's mean as hell and won't mind killing a woman. Be careful, honey! Take your time and keep out of sight."

I thought I heard her cry out, but I couldn't be certain. Just about then, Donelson must have decided to make his try, for he came out from under the wagon, running straight as an arrow toward old Pop, his gun spurting flame and smoke. He screamed something, but I couldn't hear the words.

Then Donelson's revolver snapped on an empty chamber. I

watched him trying frantically to reload as the old man's horse bore down on him. Sunlight glinted off of the hatchet he held high in the air. My hatchet! I'd left it with him when I taken off. Whirling the hatchet, he charged the bigger man head on. Donelson threw the pistol at him and made an attempt to duck, but it was too late. Shrieking his war cry, the old man slashed down with the hatchet, shearing off the killer's left ear and sinking the blade deeply into his neck. Donelson screamed, and one hand clutched at the wound in his neck as the other reached out for support and found nothing. He screamed again and went up on his toes, poised there for an instant, and then fell headlong. His body twitched once and then lay still.

The old man made a running dismount from his horse, and I watched as he ran the blade around Donelson's scalp and in one swift jerk ripped it from his head. Holding it high in the air, he yelled triumphantly and began to prance around the dead man in a victory dance, skinny legs pumping and shoulders jerking in a spasmodic rhythm.

After he'd circled the body several times, he stopped and looked down. As if inspired, he knelt down and pounded the hatchet's blunt end against Donelson's mouth. A moment later he stood up with something in his palm. The tooth! The golden tooth! He'd made a trophy out of Donelson's tooth.

CHAPTER 16

THE OLD MAN PRIED ME OUT OF THE ROCK-WALLED trap, but not without help from one who'd left and then decided to ride back to make sure I escaped. Soon as he'd calmed down some and quit doing his war dance, he clawed his way up the boulders and peered down at me. "Heyo, Jeke! What you do down dere? Bad mans all dead. I kill! You see?" He waved his bloody black-haired trophy, and his wrinkled face was all smiles.

"I know," I told him. "I saw it all, Pop. You were some kind of man out there, and I thank you for it. Now, how's about gittin' me outta here. Where's Nell? She can help us move them rocks. It won't take but one or two, and the rest won't matter. I can climb on over 'em. Where is she, Pop?"

He quit smiling and looked away. "I see she go 'way. I sorree, Jeke. I . . ." He ran out of words and shrugged.

"I understand, Pop. Listen. Go unhook the team from the wagon and bring 'em over here." I thought a moment. "Wait jest a minute, Pop. Do you know anythin' about harness? We might jest be in trouble if you don't." He nodded, but the look on his face wasn't all that reassuring.

"Thet's fine, Pop, but mebbe I better explain. Look down under the seat. You'll find a drawbar there. A piece about this long." I spread my arms to give him some idea of what to look for. I couldn't see how he could miss it.

"All right! Now, when you unhook the team, leave both of the singletrees; jest unhook them from the evener." I began to wonder if it was going to work. He was just staring at me, and I doubted that he even understood the words, much less what to look for. So I patiently explained what each piece of equipment looked like, why it was there, and how we needed to use it. Finally, I saw comprehension in his eyes, and I breathed a sigh of relief. "I come back, Jeke. You wait."

I had to smile. What else could I do? Suddenly I had to laugh, even though it hurt my head when I did. Thinking back over the last three weeks and all the real trouble I'd gotten into, this was no problem at all. Leastways there'd be nobody shooting at me; just a simple matter of moving the boulders, and I'd be out slicker'n grease.

I heard the horses coming and peered over the barricade. Pop was there, all right, but so was Nell! It was Nell that had Mollie and Jobe in hand, with the traces dragging on the ground and the singletrees hooked to the drawbar. No smile on her face, just a look of grim determination as she talked to the team and urged them along. I saw the whip tucked under her right thumb, so I reckoned she was ready for an argument if the horses showed any signs of balking.

"You came back," I said. "Why'd you run off, Nell? Hope you ain't still mad at me. I didn't mean nothin' by what I said back there. Honest! I jest know thet folks can be the cruelest when you least expect it, and I was jest tryin' to avoid gittin' you hurt. I love you, Nell! You know thet."

I might as well have talked to a stone wall. It was like she didn't even hear me. She stopped the team in close and looked up at me. "How do we do this, Jake? I can handle my end, but I don't know where to begin." She paused. "Your head is bleeding, Jake. Are you badly hurt? You look worse than before, and your face is so white." She started to say something else, but her voice died, and she looked away.

Well . . . What the heck could I say? Seemed like she'd no more interest in me, not even as a friend. What she was going to do now, you'd do for most anybody. That is, if you'd just stumbled over them, and they were in a peck of trouble, like I was. Hell! I'd help a stray dog out of a tight like that. It wasn't no more'n common decency.

"You'll need a piece of chain," I told her. "There's one length in the back of the wagon, and it oughta be enough. A piece about twenty feet long. Have Pop go and git it."

A few minutes later, he was back with the chain. I asked them to give it to me, and after they did, I passed it around the biggest boulder, the one on top of the pile. I made another wrap, which formed a clove hitch, and made darned sure the chain couldn't slip off the stone.

"Jest hook thet chain onto your drawbar," I told her. "I reckon you can figger it out from there."

Nell did as I directed and moved the team into position. A few encouraging words, and the horse leaned into the collars. Nothing happened! A few more words, and when the big stone didn't move, Nell hollered some unladylike words and popped that whip right between the horses' ears. Not really bad words, but some I'd never expected to hear from her.

That did the trick. I heard a slight scraping sound, and the rock began to move. Ever so slightly at first, and then it tilted forward and crashed to the ground.

"Thet's fine," I hollered. "I can git out now." What I really meant was that I could try. My shoulder had stiffened up considerably, and my head ached something fierce. I managed to crawl over the barrier and fall to the ground in a heap.

Pop was right there waiting. He helped me to my feet, which was a real chore in itself, as I could barely stand. "Take me over to the crick," I told him. "If I can stick my head in thet water, I figger I'll be all right. Where's Nell? Where are you, girl? Right now, I need your help, and I need it bad!"

"I'm right here, Jake. Behind you." Her voice sounded a lot different, like maybe she was about ready to cry. Turning, I staggered and almost fell. She reached forward, and I had her in my arms. "Don't ever go away again, my darlin' Nell. I'm sorry I said those things, and I'll never say 'em again. Not ever! Forgive me, Nell. Say you forgive me!''

Her arms were around me now, and she was hanging on. We kissed, and I tasted the salt of her tears and mine. Heard her say she loved me too, and there was nothing to forgive.

Gently, she disengaged herself and stepped back. "First we must talk, Jake, but not until I've taken care of you. I have some things in a parfleche on my horse. The Old One is getting them out, so let's go over to the wagon." She taken hold of my hand and put her other arm around my shoulders.

I wasn't feeling too well, I have to admit that. Sorta sick to my stomach and dizzier than an old coot. She helped me walk to the wagon and sat me down on the tongue. Pop brought the skin pouch and set it down beside Nell. He was looking mighty anxious but didn't know what the heck to do.

By that time she realized I'd been shot in the shoulder and had that bullet graze on my leg. Neither one was really serious, but they'd get much worse if not cared for.

The wound on my head was the worst. The ball had struck solidly just in back of one ear and flattened as it glanced off my skull but stayed under the skin. Nell found this out as she examined me. I'd naturally thought it had passed on after knocking me down. She guided my hand, and it could be felt, all right, a lump about the size of a pea that I found under the short hairs on the back of my head.

"It must come out," she told me. "Otherwise, it will become inflamed, and you could be very sick, maybe even sicker than before. I wish we had some whiskey to wash out such an ugly wound, but we'll have to be content with hot water."

"Look in the back of the wagon, Nell. I meant it to be a surprise, but I reckon you won't mind. It ain't rum, but it sure packs a powerful punch."

The keg was small and held only two gallons, but she was smiling as she brought it to me. "You remembered the story I told," she said. "About my grandmother and her wonderful bride price. You remembered!" She seemed very pleased.

"Thet ain't all," I told her. "Reach up there on the wagon seat. The rifle! Bring it down. Ain't it a pretty one? I meant it for you, but now I have to do somethin' else. If you'd ask the old man to step over here, I'd be obliged."

She called out, and Pop came hustling over. When he seen that rifle, his face lit up, and he stood there waiting.

I looked him square in the eyes and spoke up. "This is a rifle for a brave man, Tset-a-go-hn. It's yours, and I only wish I had more to give. Take it, please, and use it for whatever you wish. It's a chief's gun, and you're the bravest chief I ever knowed. You've really earned this rifle."

Well sir, his face was something to see. He taken that in his hands and rubbed it all over, jabbering away in Apache, and likely telling me how happy he was to get it. I said to look on the wagon seat and take the flask and mold that he would find there.

"Thank you, Jake," Nell said. "I'll make him a fine cover for the rifle. Use doeskin and lots of beads. You just made him the happiest man in the world."

She was right. He was starry-eyed as he walked away. I had meant every word, of course. He had done a mighty brave thing. Took real nerve to charge at Donelson with him firing that Navy Colt. He'd had no trouble hitting me, and the old man had been mighty lucky.

CHAPTER 17

~~~~~~

In spite of Nell's careful cleaning of my wounds, I was a mighty sick man for a few days. The head wound festered, and I ran a high fever, but finally it came down, and I began to recover. She and Pop had made a comfortable camp alongside the creek, and the old man kept us supplied with a lot of fresh meat. He loved that rifle and spent hours just fondling it and polishing the inlays with a piece of leather.

I'd told them both about meeting up with Elon Westermarck in Silver City and lending him the money for supplies. The mine would be half ours, I said, and we'd work it until we had enough money to buy a place of our own.

Nell was filling out even more, and I knew it couldn't be much longer before the baby came. I talked about how proud I'd be. Said I hoped it would be a boy, naturally, but that there wasn't nothing wrong with having a baby girl. When we were alone, Nell was affectionate, but I could see that something was bothering her. She was holding something bottled up inside, and I wondered. A couple of times I asked what was on her mind, but she either couldn't or wouldn't say.

Finally, I was all healed up and feeling stronger every day. We'd been taking short walks along that creek and had worked together moving the animals to where we could find better graze. I was eager to get to the mine and start digging, so I pushed to break camp. We were coming back from a walk when I chose to pop the question.

"Will you marry me, Nell? We can go to Fort Bayard so's the chaplain can git it done right and then head up for the mine. What do you say, honey? Will you marry me?"

She turned and faced me, and her eyes were solemn. "I'm sorry, Jake," she said. "We can't ever be married. Now you are well again, and able to travel on your own. It is time for us to say good-bye. Let's say it now while we are still good friends. Later on you may not feel as you do now."

It was like I'd just been struck by lightning! Hard as I tried, I couldn't open my mouth or speak a word. There she was, telling me we couldn't never be married. Standing next to me, with her beautiful eyes fixed on mine, and saying she couldn't be my wife. No explanation. No nothing!

Suddenly I had to get away. Had to be as far away as I could possibly get, where I'd never see her ever again. She just stood there, waiting. Then I got real mad. If she'd made up her mind for whatever reason, then to hell with all the plans I'd made! To hell with her! To hell with it all!

"Aren't you going to ask me why, Jake?" Her voice was low-pitched, and she was staring at the ground. "Don't you want to know my reasons? I'll tell you if you wish."

I shook my head, not daring to trust my voice. There was a lump in my throat big enough to choke a horse, and to even breathe was a chore. I couldn't have said a word if my life had depended on it. Not right then. I'd been a damn fool! I'd taken too much for granted and tried to stampede this woman into marrying me without thinking it out first. What could her reasons be? I didn't know, and I wasn't all that minded to find out. She *had* told me she loved me. That was a true fact. But that didn't mean she wanted to be my wife. Right then, I couldn't stay another moment. I had to leave.

It taken me only minutes to gather in the horses and lead

them to the wagon. Half an hour later, I was heading out of camp, with old Pop staring after me. He'd asked why I wanted to leave, but I still couldn't say a word. I reckon that he must've known what was happening, because he didn't push. I shook his hand before I climbed up and told him I'd like him to take care of her. That maybe we'd see each other one of these days. Then I drove off.

Westermarck was tickled to death to see me show up. He'd been worried when I didn't turn up as promised. I said as little as possible. Told him about the trouble I'd had with Donelson but didn't go into the details.

For the next six months we worked double shifts. It was hard work but mighty rewarding. Steadily, the gold we were stock-piling increased until we had to find another place to hide it. Seldom did we see anyone, except for an occasional down-on-his-luck prospector. Then a patrol came by, and my friend Lieutenant Waggonier was leading it. I was really happy to see him again, and me 'n' Elon threw them a big feed. I'd had the luck to shoot two deer just the day before, and we gave them all a meal to remember.

Afterwards, Waggonier and I were off by ourselves, and he asked me about Nell. Wondered why I was off in that lonely, desolate spot when I could be with the girl I loved. I had to get it off my chest, had to tell someone what had happened, no matter what. I hadn't been able to speak of it with Westermarck. He was a nice feller, and we got along, but he was different some-how. A city feller, he hadn't ever faced a blizzard, caught on horseback, twenty miles from the nearest shelter. Never had to outrun a herd of stampeding cows or fight off a pack of hostiles who outnumbered him ten to one. Neither had Waggonier, I reckoned, but he was a horseback soldier, and somehow there was a difference.

So we sat down on a log, and I told him the whole story. Sat there and bared my soul while he puffed away on a pipe and lis-tened. He let me tell the whole tale before he said a word. A fine, understanding feller, that lieutenant.

"So that's how I stood when she came right down to tellin'

me," I concluded. "Jest another dumb cowhand who lacked the brains that God gave a goose. I was so durn sure of myself, certain that all I had to do was ask, and she would jump at the chance. I sure found out different," I told him ruefully. "She didn't want no part of me!"

He knocked out his pipe against his palm. "I'm not all that sure she didn't," he told me. "From what you'd told me before, this woman had gone through a terrible experience. A *white* man had murdered her husband and tried to kill you in your bed. I'm no doctor, but I'd say she might just be confused in her mind. She identifies you as both victor and a victim, and that's bound to be confusing. She can't believe that any white man is to be trusted, yet she sees herself in love with you. Add to that the fact that she is carrying a baby for the first time, and you see an emotionally confused lady. Her standards are all turned around.

"Women are wonderful and complex creatures, Jake. No man will ever completely understand them. They feel things that we will never feel. They regard things in a different light than us. Their values are more basic, and they fear change. That—" He held up his finger. "That is the key to your problem, I believe. Tell me. Do you still love this woman and want her to be your wife?" I nodded, and he went on.

"You must somehow show her that you are no different than she is. You mentioned something about a bride's price? Her grandmother, I believe. Something about twenty horses? The answer is there, or so I believe. Trust me, Jake. Do that! Leave here tomorrow and come to the fort with me. I can't promise for sure, but I think we can sell you a few horses."

"I think I see what you mean, Lieutenant, but I haven't a ghost of an idea where to look for her. Far as I know, they might have gone across the border and into Old Mexico."

He smiled and then laughed out loud. "I know exactly, Jake. I can take you to their camp any time. My coming here was no accident. Surely you must have sensed that. I want to see them settled, and what better way to do it? Besides, I consider you a friend, and I'd like to see you work things out. Maybe I'll be looking for a ranch job someday."

Early the next morning, I packed my stuff and said good-bye to Westermarck. "The mine's all yours now," I said to him. "You won't have no trouble with nobody now thet we've established the claim. Besides, the lieutenant will keep an eye on the place, so you jest holler if you need help. You take care now, you hear? Soon's I get me a place, I'll let you know where it is. The latchstring will always be there where you can reach it. So long, Elon. Thanks for helping when I needed it." We shook hands, and I turned away.

CHAPTER 18

NELL AND POP HAD PICKED OUT A MIGHTY PRETTY place. A box canyon up in the northwest corner of the Burro Mountains, it had a fair-sized creek that looked to be year-round and an almighty fine crop of thick grass. I was all decked out for courting, with my buckskins fresh and clean and my bunch of fine horses running ahead of me. No scrubs at all, just big geldings that'd run over a thousand pounds. In time, they could be sold off, and we'd buy some breeding stock.

I reckon they'd seen me coming from way off, because both came out to meet me. Nell smiled, but she was wondering how I'd found them and why I had come. Pop was happier'n a pig let to root in an apple barrel, and he jabbered away for all he was worth. They led the way up to their camp and invited me to light and set a spell. I never paid no mind to the mystified Nell but kept up a running conversation with Pop. I was not sure he could understand all of it, and I know I had trouble understanding his lingo, but I just kept on talking.

Finally, we sat down, and I put my saddlebags close by my side. They both looked at them curious-like, Pop seated on the other side of the fire and Nell off to one side. Opening a pocket, I brought out two brand-new pipes with long, straight stems. The bowls were carved to look like a bull's head, with short horns and chin whiskers. I held both up in the air and then presented one to Pop with a flourish. He thanked me and brought out his tobacco sack. We filled the pipes and lit them from the fire. I taken a long pull and puffed the smoke up in the air slowly.

Nell finally spoke up. "Why are you here, Jake? There is no reason for your coming. I made up my mind, and I will never change it. You heard my decision."

I ignored her and spoke to Pop about the weather. "Sure look's like we'll have an early summer, don't it? Not a lot of rain last winter, but the grass seems to be holdin' its own. How've you been in here? Was it a rough winter? Have any problems with findin' meat? I seen eight big deer as I was ridin' in, and all of 'em were in good flesh."

Poor old Pop. He wasn't sure what was going on but must have had some idea, so he went along with it. "I like smoke pipe, Jeke. Good pipe! Good smoke! You like?"

I nodded. "I 'spect you're wonderin' why I'm here. We left each other sorta sudden-like last year, and I couldn't git a chance to tell you what was on my mind. Now, I would like to have your daughter-in-law, Pop. I know she's hard to git along with and has a habit of bossin' folks, but I come prepared to handle thet. I figger what she needs is a real good beatin' every now and then. You know! So's she knows her place. Nothin' severe, you understand, just a touch now and then with a willow switch.

"Now, I've brought in thirty head of the finest horses a man could ever wish for, and they are all yours. You won't have to lift a finger takin' care of 'em, because I'll do it for you as part of the deal. We'll be partners in a sorta way, and we'll split everythin' right down the middle. Now, how does thet sound to you, Tset-a-go-hn? Have we got us an out-and-out trade? My horses for your daughter-in-law."

"Oh, no you don't, Mister Bailey!" Nell was outraged, and her face was something to see. "You aren't bringing in your horses and trading them off for me. Who do you think I am, anyway? I'm no chattel to be traded off for horses, and in no case would I accept you for a husband!''

Pop had finally caught on, and he was grinning from ear to ear. He nodded vigorously. ''Yes, Jeke! You take, now! No listen she. I am same fadder, and I give you she.'' With a big grin on his face, he stood up and gave me his hand.

Nell ran around the fire and caught me a good one. Fist doubled up, she smacked me right in the face! I caught her and held her in close as she beat on my chest with both of her fists. ''You're no better than the rest,'' she blubbered. ''Nothing but a big bully who won't take no for an answer. I told you we could never marry, and I had a reason. Why have you come here? I've been trying to . . .'' She began to cry on my shoulder, her sobs muffled by the buckskin shirt.

''There, there, now, honey. I love you more than anyone in the world, and I want you for my wife. I told you thet a long time ago. Now, think of it. Thirty horses! A bigger bride price than even your grandmother got! I'd have brung some rum, a whole big keg, but it ain't any easier to get.''

She raised her head and looked up at me, her lovely eyes filled with tears. She smiled a little uncertainly, but at least it was a smile. ''You do love me, don't you, Jake? And it is a wonderful bride price, I guess. But you're white, and the two of us will never make a go of it. I just know we won't. Go away! Take your horses and go away from here! No! The horses are enough, Jake. I love you, and I guess we can try to make our marriage work. I'll marry you, Jake.''

So that's how it all began. Now we have eight children, five boys and three girls. The ranch covers over a hundred thousand acres, and it's all paid for. Every now and then I catch her looking at me, and I have to smile. She still has her doubts, even after all these years.

AUTHOR'S COMMENTARY

The Native Americans in this story were variously known as Mimbreños Apaches, Coppermine Apaches, Ojo Calientes Apaches, Gila Apaches, and Mimbres Apaches. I have chosen to use the latter term, Mimbres Apaches. A literal translation would be Willow People, *mimbres* being a Spanish word. They knew themselves as the Shis-Inday, or the People of the Woods. *Apache* is a French word meaning "savage," but they were savage only in their fight to defend the land they knew as home. They had a deep love for their children and taught them to be brave and strong. They were a virtuous people who abhorred the act of rape and normally married only within their race. They were clean, honorable, and intelligent people who didn't steal or lie. They never tortured a prisoner. Yet they had to suffer great hardships. The Mexican government paid a bounty of two hundred pesos for a male scalp and one hundred fifty for that of a female or a child. Between 1846 and 1866 the estimated number of Apaches dropped from seven thousand to less than sixteen hundred because of this barbaric custom, and the Mimbres represented only two hundred of this pitiful remnant. We owe the Shis-Inday a great debt. One we will never repay!

Robert Vaughn Bell
Creek Park Ranch

ABOUT THE AUTHOR

A true Westerner by birth, Robert Vaughn Bell grew up in the Nebraska cattle country. Bell has written extensively about the Old West in magazine and newspaper articles and in his previous five Western novels, all published by Ballantine. He and his wife, Billie, reside on their Creek Park Ranch, high in the foothills of the California Sierras, where they raise beef cattle and continue research for his books.